KU-144-786

REVENGE COMES LATE

When two young gaolbirds were at last released, they had but one thought in mind — to seek revenge against the man who had betrayed them. However, the flame of vengeance is fickle, and sparks from it can alight wherever the tinder of resentment is dry and waiting, setting the land into a sudden conflagration. So it was in that hot summer, when old wounds reopened and guns blazed to settle old scores. Many were drawn into the smoke and flame of the final battle, but such was the carnage that few would emerge unscathed.

Books by Bill Morrison
in the Linford Western Library:

THE WOODEN GUN
A DOLLAR FROM THE STAGE
CHEYENNE NOON
RIVER GOLD
DESERT DUEL

BILL MORRISON

REVENGE
COMES LATE

WARWICKSHIRE
COUNTY LIBRARY

CONTROL No.

Complete and Unabridged

LINFORD
Leicester

First published in Great Britain in 2004 by
Robert Hale Limited
London

First Linford Edition
published 2005
by arrangement with
Robert Hale Limited
London

The moral right of the author
has been asserted

Copyright © 2004 by Bill Morrison
All rights reserved

British Library CIP Data

Morrison, Bill, *1931 –*
    Revenge comes late.—Large print ed.—
Linford western library
1. Western stories
2. Large type books
I. Title
823.9'14 [F]

ISBN 1–84395–917–8

Published by
F. A. Thorpe (Publishing)
Anstey, Leicestershire

Set by Words & Graphics Ltd.
Anstey, Leicestershire
Printed and bound in Great Britain by
T. J. International Ltd., Padstow, Cornwall

This book is printed on acid-free paper

1

Sam stood outside and blinked up at the sky. He had looked up at the sun almost every day over the past ten years but now it was as if he was seeing it for the first time, even though he had spent long days and weeks labouring under its sweltering heat in the fields with an iron around his ankle.

He had looked forward to this moment every day of his imprisonment — when he had dared to — for often enough this moment of his longed for release had been too painful an idea to bear, especially at the start, when it had seemed a million miles away.

But now he felt kind of disappointed — the moment flat, like it meant nothing. He could not explain it. He felt empty, like a water-melon with its inside scooped out and just a dry shell remaining. He guessed that was what prison did to you over the years as it ripped your guts out from day to day until there wasn't much feeling left and all hope was squashed out of you.

Even so it was a kind of relief. He had made it! He had worked his way out of the place and he could walk away without being challenged or hit with a cudgel. Just the same, he did not dare to look behind at the grim building. He had the feeling it might drag him back into its dark interior and the sun would disappear. Instead he glanced sideways at Thady, who stood in silence like himself, blinking, but with the twist of a wry smile on his lips.

Thady made a strange-looking figure. It was queer seeing him back in his old clothes instead of the prison outfit. The rugged features looked just the same, with his prominent cheekbones and tight mouth, though his red hair was sparser and there were deep lines now in his face that had not been there before the jail had carved them into him. His old clothes still fitted him pretty well too, though he was now thirty-five years old instead of the twenty-five he had been when he last wore them.

It wasn't just like that with Sam. Ten years in jail could make a hell of a big change to a fifteen-year-old as he went forward into adulthood. None of his old stuff had fitted at all so they had rigged him out with an old shirt and jacket, old pants and boots, from inmates who hadn't been able to hold out long enough to get them back on release. The fit was bad but it was better than nothing and he just had to try to forget about their previous owners.

'You men looking for somewhere to stay?' The little charity woman was by their side once again, smiling with a lack of conviction, as though she felt it was her duty but took no pleasure it. Her tiny blue eyes were on Sam because he was the better-looking of the two ex-convicts, with his youthful, round features and black hair, still with its prison crop. 'We may be able to find you temporary lodgings.'

'It's OK, ma'am,' cut in Thady. 'We got somewheres to go.'

It was a lie but Sam knew Thady had other plans. He wanted to push on without waste of time and without being held back by interfering old ladies. Sam told himself he was of the same mind.

'That's right, ma'am,' he confirmed, 'but thanks for the money. That was very good of you and your charity.'

She had given them two dollars each as was usual when men were released. It was a way of helping them to make a fresh start and maybe leading them towards a more Christian life. Some hint of relief came into her eyes at their answer. It meant she could go home for today — her duty done.

'Well, no sense in hanging around,' grunted Thady. 'Let's get on our way.'

He began walking up the dusty road without a backward glance at the woman. Sam nodded to her with an attempt at politeness and caught up with Thady within a few strides. They were about the same height now and of similar build. Prison work had put muscle on Sam and the years had grown him well above his companion's shoulder-level where he had been before the law slammed the gates on them both. At that time he had really looked up to Thady in more senses than one, but now it wasn't exactly like that. There had been a change in his ways of thinking and he could see into the older man in ways he could not before.

They were heading north. It was the only way to go. North had been in Thady's mind ever since he read the newspaper five years ago. Always it was 'north'. He would head *north* and find Lewis and finish him for good.

Sam was not against the idea. His hatred of Lewis ran about as deep as did that of Thady. Still, after ten years, what was the use of breaking into a sprint?

'Maybe we ought to get some grub with the money,' he suggested. 'There must be a store in the township back there — only a couple of miles on the other side of the penitentiary. We need to eat on the way.'

'Naw, there'll be a place not much further on. We kin git somethin' there. I went up this way a couple of times with the chaingang. I'm pretty sure of it. Quicker I git my hands on that son-of-a-bitch the better . . . for me, not for him!'

A mile later, though, and he stopped in the hot sunlight, wiping his brow, and growling that those polecats in the prison had stolen his hat. Sam remembered neither had worn hats at the time of their arrest, having lost them in the robbery, but did not say so. They sat in silence for a few minutes, then Thady pulled a scrap of crumpled newspaper out of his pocket. He read it again for about the thousandth time.

'Red Lance,' he breathed, 'near this place called Red Lance . . . '

'That's it,' agreed Sam, having read it himself more than once. 'Goddamned township called Red Lance. Near there, anyhow, that right? But where the hell's Red Lance?'

'We'll find it. Listen, here, listen to what it says: 'The new mine at Red Lance, known as the Starlight mine, is making a handsome profit and is set to make even more as a fresh silver lode has been uncovered. The owner, Mr Thomas Lewis, expressed his delight in the new find and stated that all his investment and hard work were really paying off. He plans to take on more men within a few weeks and can offer work to any man with the required experience . . . '

'Yeah, I know, I've read it,' grunted Sam.

'Investment and hard work! Blasted, thievin' polecat! That's all our money — or ought to be!'

'You're right,' replied Sam, but with a little less conviction than he would have had years ago. 'He was a dirty double-dealer, no question!'

He sat and stared at his dusty

footwear, feeling suddenly despondent. All around the country was barren, except for a few shrubs here and there and dry grasses blowing in the hot breeze. The trail led into the distance, rutted with the passage of wagons and farm carts, but looking as if it went nowhere. To follow it seemed like going nowhere. Maybe there was nowhere to go . . .

'This here township you're talking about,' he said at last. 'How far is it?'

'Not so far. We'll git there. See that goddamned skunk, when I git him.'

'Come on,' said Sam, rising. 'There's no good sitting around in this heat. We need some shelter and something to eat and drink. Let's go.'

They went on but there was no township. Thady's memory had not served him well on that. When eventually the sun slipped quickly below the horizon, they slumped exhausted on the bare ground. Thady fell almost at once into a snoring slumber. Sam was not so lucky. He slept only fitfully the whole night long, turning restlessly on the hard sandy soil and staring up to a star-spangled sky.

This was his first night of freedom. It wasn't anything like he had expected. He had no clear idea of what he might have expected or hoped for but he knew it was nothing like this.

Bitterness came into his heart. It seemed as if he had spent all his life in jail or running like hell from the law or being knocked around by his old man or being scowled at by old ladies. It was all a mix-up and he had never got anything out of it. His mind drifted, as it had done countless times before, on his earlier life; losing his mother and being left with a drunken, brutal father, then running off and taking up with guys like Thady, who were not all that much different from himself, but saw a solution to life's hardships by taking what they could and not worrying too much about other people. He himself had fallen in with such ideas and Thady had made a pretty good friend. They had shared whatever they stole with one another and sometimes even smoked the same old pipe and drank beer out of the same bottle.

It was when they met up with Lewis that things had really got out of hand. Lewis was a smart feller in a way. He wore a suit he had picked up someplace and liked to comb his long, black hair in the mornings. It was his idea to rob that little bank and he had got horses from a wedding party, where they had been left hitched up securely enough but unattended. He had sent Thady and Sam in to do the robbing while he kept watch outside and waited for the money to be passed out. They only had one gun between them, which Lewis kept in his belt, but he had made a couple of replicas out of birch wood which looked just like the real thing. Thady and Sam had gone in with them and, sure enough, had scared hell out of the two women and the man behind the counter. The bag of cash and notes had been handed over without argument.

They had run out then and thrown the bag up to Lewis in the saddle. They turned to mount their own horses only to find they had been unhitched and had wandered off down the street. Then Lewis had fired at Thady but his restless horse had made him miss and the bullet had thumped into the wall. After that, everything seemed all mixed up, with people shouting and screaming as citizens realized what was happening. Many came running out of their houses, waving rifles and handguns but too late to stop Lewis from making a good getaway.

Then came the dark days of the trial when there was much talk of hanging both of them. They escaped that fate because they had no guns so nobody could say it was an armed robbery. Anyhow nobody got hurt and it was Lewis who had finished up stealing the money.

But it was anger and hatred and the need for revenge against Lewis that had kept them going in that hell of a prison.

Daily, Thady had vowed to kill the double-crosser as soon as he got out. Once he had become so mad that he had almost kicked a hole in the cement of the cell wall until a warder had come in and hit him with a club. Sam, too, had had his visions of getting a gun from somewhere and shooting Lewis, who had obviously planned from the start to have all the loot for himself and to kill his partners so they could be of no further trouble to him. That was what Lewis had figured all along. Nevertheless, always — even in the worst days — they had reckoned on turning things round and had seen the light of vengeance at the end of the tunnel.

Sam was still awake and staring at the sky when the sun came up. He rose to his feet, slowly and stiffly, and looked at the track still stretching into the distance. He was aware of a sense of depression made worse by his hunger and terrible thirst. Thady awoke and tried to spit but could not. He attempted to say something about getting even with Lewis but the words did not get past his cracked lips.

'Come on,' grunted Sam, 'let's go.'

At about noon they saw the wagon up ahead. It had come to a stop but even so it was a while before their shambling, exhausted gait brought them near. There was a grey-haired man unloading boxes and placing them laboriously at the side of the trail. When he saw them he straightened up stiffly and stood, staring suspiciously, his lined, tanned features set in suspense.

'Howdy!' said Sam, raising his hand in a gesture of friendship. There was no reply. The elderly man retained his air of tense suspicion. Sam could understand it. He didn't know them any better than a rattlesnake under a log.

'Looks like you got trouble,' went on Sam, his eyes on the left fore-wheel of the wagon, which was stuck in a deep hole. 'Maybe we kin help?'

The old sharp eyes, cold grey in colour, searched them all over, seeming to look for concealed weapons, then relaxed a little.

'Sure,' he answered. 'You kin help.'

He walked round to the front of the wagon where the team of two horses, well fed and watered by the look of them, waited patiently for word to move on. He pulled a long pole out from under the canvas and handed it to Thady.

'This here's just the thing to lever it up, only it takes a bit of heavin'. I'm getting a little past my prime and don't find it so easy these days.'

'Thing is,' said Thady, finding his voice, 'we need a drink real bad and something to eat.'

'I kin see that. You kin have a drink but the grub comes later — if you earn it.'

The tepid water from the canteen worked wonders and the task turned out to be easier than it looked. They shoved the long pole under the wagon, put their shoulders under it and straightened up, muscles straining, until the rim of the wheel was about even with the edge of the hole and the old man could lead the team forward a little until all was clear.

'That's it,' said Thady. 'Now kin we eat?'

The old man brought out some stale bread and cheese and a piece of pork and they ate ravenously, sitting in the shade of the wagon. He eyed them closely.

'You guys got names?'

'Sure,' said Sam, his mouth full. 'This here's Thady Ryan. I'm Sam — Sam Witchell. Thanks for the grub, mister.'

'Karl Plinston, that's me,' came the response.

The old man seemed more confident and it was not just because they had helped with the wheel. From his seated position, Sam could see the bulge of a handgun under his jacket.

'You two on the trail, looking for work or something?'

'Yeah,' replied Thady. He squinted thoughtfully at the sky and then looked directly at the old man. 'Mining — we're into mining. Know of any mines up ahead or anywheres?'

The old man grinned for the first time. He glanced at Thady's hands. They were tough all right — but from breaking stones in prison, not from mining.

'You guys just out of jail?'

They were silent, then Thady shook his head.

'What the hell makes you say that?'

'Them haircuts. Nobody has hair like that except cons. You look like what you are.'

'OK,' put in Sam, 'but we got discharged regular. We got our discharge papers.' He pulled his out from under his shirt. 'We ain't runaways or anything.'

Karl examined the paper and handed it back with a nod. There came a hint of sympathy into his eyes.

'That's fine. I ain't trying to accuse you of anythin'. Only, if you're on the look-out for work, you ain't likely to find any. Men jest out of prison don't inspire much confidence. But I could use your help for a few days. I got boxes and stuff to shift around a bit and I need a rest from the team at times.'

'Sure, that would suit us!' agreed Sam, brightly.

'If you're heading north, OK,' said Thady. 'What about pay?'

'What you need to eat and no more — and when we git to parts where the trail goes uphill, you git out and walk. Take it or leave it. If I think you deserve any pay, you'll be dealt with, fair and square.'

'We'll take it,' put in Sam quickly, before Thady could speak.

'One thing more,' said the old man. 'I got my daughter in the wagon too. You keep clear of her. That understood?'

They opened their eyes wide in surprise. There had been no sound from the wagon except that of a box falling over when they heaved on the pole. As if she had heard her father's words, a girl appeared from under the canvas at the front. She was black-haired and pretty and wore a simple cotton dress and a little waistcoat of the kind favoured by Mexican women.

Sam caught her eyes, dark and beautiful, and opened his mouth to speak, until he saw the suspicion and hostility which was there, and noted the long knife in its sheath, hanging at her narrow waist. He saw too that her left arm seemed stiff and slow of movement as she picked up a small hat-box which had somehow fallen into the dirt.

'This here's Julia,' said Karl, 'A fine girl if ever there was one and — as for me,' he went on, grey eyes staring at them down his long nose and seeming to bore into their minds, 'I'm the finest travelling doctor in the whole of Texas!'

2

A couple of days later Thady sat on the buckboard, driving the team, while Sam relaxed beside him, leaning back and yawning. Inside the wagon the old man slept uncomfortably in the heat which even the heavy canvas could not much reduce. At the rear the girl looked back along the trail and sometimes forward to where the two younger men exchanged a few remarks in low tones.

'Crazy set-up, ain't it?' whispered Thady, keeping his voice under the level of the slow plod of the team's hoofs and the rattling of the wagon. 'This 'medicine man' and 'snake-oil man' kind of business ... wagon stacked with crates, full of medicine and stuff ... '

'Yeah, could be, though, that it does sick people some good. Regular doctors cost a lot and there ain't too many around in some parts.'

'Sure, likely makes plenty money at it too . . . What do you reckon?'

'Don't know,' answered Sam, hesitantly, not liking the turn in the conversation.

Thady left it at that, fearing to be overheard, and snapped the reins to move the tiring animals on.

'Go easy on them critters.' Karl seemed to have roused himself and to be taking a fresh interest in his surroundings. 'Better pull up and give them a drink. Don't want them caving in on me.'

Thady did as commanded and Sam went round to give the team a leather bucket of water. The girl had descended from the wagon and had walked a little way down the track, busy with her own thoughts.

'Next place we get to is Fairmount,' said Karl. 'Jest about five miles, I reckon. Maybe do a bit of business there. Tell you what, you two git the boards up around the wagon, while I git myself ready. Hey, Julia, better git yourself fixed up for consultations! Soon be there!'

They disappeared into the wagon while Sam and Thady hung the long wooden boards around the outside, covered with slogans like: MARVELLOUS MODERN MEDICINE! — CAST YOUR ILLS AWAY FOR GOOD HEALTH HAS COME TO STAY! and WONDERFUL CURES FROM ALL THE CORNERS OF THE EARTH!

They grinned with amusement as they hung the boards into position. After completing the task according to the instructions given, they sat at the side of the trail in the shade of a straggling bush.

'I could do with a beer,' complained Thady. 'Ain't had that for years! God, what would I give for a big, cool, delicious beer!'

'You'll get it in time,' promised Sam cheerfully.

'The old feller's handed out nothin''

but water and coffee,' went on Thady. 'Bet he has some liquor in that wagon and . . . ' he sat up suddenly but lowered his voice, 'money too . . . Bet he has a sackful of dollars hidden in there someplace.'

'Could be . . . '

'Them horses could take us where we want to go a sight faster than this.'

'They're trained for the team, not as saddle horses.'

'They'd be all right. I used to ride bare-back when I was a kid.'

'That wasn't yesterday.'

'We could get saddles with the money . . . and them two guns that the old feller and the girl have — the rifle and the Colt — would give us somethin' to help settle things with Lewis.'

'That ain't right! Them folks has been good to us! I'm as keen as you are to fix Lewis but there's a right way and a wrong way. Turning the rattlesnake on them is the wrong way.'

'We'll never git even with that Lewis polecat by playing Sunday

School, for Christ's sake!'

'Take it easy. We'll git him.' Sam turned to glance at his companion. He noticed that Thady was developing a twitch around the corner of his mouth when he was excited. It had been there in the prison. Now it seemed worse. 'We've been waiting a long time. Now we're on our way but I ain't doing the dirty on the old man and his daughter, no sirree!'

'You think she's really his daughter?'

'I don't know. She seems young to have such an old father, sure enough, but you kin never tell.'

'I think somethin' different!' Thady leered suddenly and spat in the dirt.

Sam tightened his lips, feeling a surge of anger, but at the same time, uncertainty.

'She ain't like that! She seems like a fine enough person to me. That ain't fair talk, Thady!'

'Fine person, eh? — and she looks at me as if I was a prairie-dog or something! Yeah? Well, what the hell, let's keep thinking about Lewis.'

Just then, Karl appeared on the buckboard. Sam and Thady gasped in amazement at the transformation. He was dressed in a black tail-coat suit and wore a smart top hat, grey silk tie and a white shirt, that gleamed in the sun. Gone was his almost white hair. His head now shone with black macassar and a fine moustache adorned his upper lip. In his hand he held a cane with a silver knob which he twirled in the air. He had lost twenty years in a matter of minutes.

He looked at them in amusement, appreciating their bewilderment.

'Always a good idea, fellers, to look professional when you're getting near a township where you're going to do business. Never know how many citizens you might meet up with on the way in. Hey, Julia, you about ready?' He stepped to the ground and approached them as Julia came from behind the canvas. She stood silently, looking over their heads as if they did not exist. They both stared, lost in admiration. Here was a beautiful Indian girl in a headdress and buckskin costume. The red paint on her cheeks seemed merely to enhance her beauty.

'That's my chief assistant,' said Karl proudly. 'She wins their hearts while I attend to their brains. Tell you what, fellers.' He turned to them as if to speak in confidence. 'I could do with a bit of help from you, too. I want you to mingle with the crowd and when I raise this hand with my fingers stretched like this, you come forward to buy whatever I'm trying to sell. You come first, Sam, then your buddy. Try to look keen and excited about it. Thing is, you see, folks are like sheep, and they don't generally like to move until somebody else moves first. Here's a couple of dollars each. Give me back the medicine when the show's over and the crowd has gone home.'

They got on their way again, this time with Karl taking the reins and the girl sitting up very straight beside him, as he wanted to attract as much attention as possible as he approached the town. Sam and Thady sat in the back under the awning. Sam's eyes wandered time and time again to the girl, watching her fine black hair drifting in the wind. She had said almost nothing to them since they had joined up with Karl. When Sam attempted to speak to her, she had answered shortly in a voice that was pleasant to hear because she could speak in no other way, but there was no hint of friendship or trust. Her eyes remained cold. Sam knew there was a deep hurt somewhere in her mind. Sure, she carried an injury of some kind in her arm, which was always stiff as if she could hardly bend it at the elbow, but there was another wound, much deeper in her soul.

At first, Sam had wondered if her hostility was just a response to the fact that they were a couple of jailbirds, not to be trusted, but he did not feel that to be the case. This was something to do with men. At least, he thought, maybe that was it. But it was so deep and hurtful that the knife had to be kept hanging at her waistband.

Thady sat at the other side of the wagon, back to the canvas wall, his eyes ranging over the wooden crates and cardboard boxes all around. Sam knew he was searching for a likely place where the old man might keep his money but there were no clues and an expression of exasperation soon spread over the rugged features. Sam controlled his anger but made up his mind to put things straight with Thady and let him know for certain that he could only set out to steal from Karl and Julia by destroying the long friendship which had endured throughout their years of imprisonment.

'Hey, Karl.' It was evident to Sam that Thady's patience was rapidly giving way as he now broached the subject he had meant to keep quiet about until at least a few more days had passed. 'You ever heard of a place called Red Lance — kind of a township, somewhere?'

Karl seemed to hesitate as if searching his memory . . . 'Yeah, I've heard of it.'

'You ever been there?'

'Yeah, once, but I jest passed through.'

'What's it like?'

'Not much of a place. Few shacks and a saloon. Injun fight there a long time ago, as far as I heard.'

'How far from here, do'ya reckon?'

'Sixty or seventy miles, maybe. Something like that. Why do you want to know about Red Lance?'

'Well . . . ' Thady's voice trailed off as he sought for an answer that wouldn't give anything away. 'Thinking about getting back to mining. Silver mine there, that right?'

'I heard tell.' Karl's chuckle was sardonic. There came a silence, then Thady asked, 'You goin' back there?'

'Nope.'

'How come?'

'Nothing to go for. No custom to speak of.'

'What about the miners? They don't need medicine?'

'Whiskey mostly — and they get that at the saloon.'

'So you ain't goin' there, nohow?'

Karl grunted as if irritated and shook his head. It seemed to Sam that Thady had said too much. Karl's mind must be turning over as he tried to figure out what this ex-con wanted so badly at the silver mine that he had to pretend to be searching so far afield for work. The old man did not believe that yarn about them having been miners before. That seemed obvious.

'It don't matter,' put in Sam, trying to smooth things out. 'We kin get work someplace.'

As the wagon approached the little town of Fairmount, they saw more and more people who stared and grinned and laughed as Karl waved to them from the wagon. Some of them, having nothing better to do, followed on behind, calling out remarks about snake-oil and guys in top hats and pretty little Injun squaws. Karl took it all in good part and led on through the main street until he came to the square beside the little timber-and-stone-built church.

It was there that he really seemed to come into his own. Gone was the bent old man, weary, cynical and tired of life. Now, he was the showman, brash and confident. He stood on a box, struck a posture, and began to extol the virtues of his medicines and cures gathered by science from the four corners of the world. He had medicine to put an end to lumbago, rheumatism, toothache, persistent headache, stomach pain, cancers, ear-inflammation, and salves to clear up wounds in half the usual time.

To begin with, only about a dozen people gathered round, but gradually the crowd grew, while the great Doctor Swigg-Hardy, as he now called himself, yelled louder by the minute.

Sam and Thady, in the crowd as

instructed, stared and listened in amazement, and when the great man's hand stretched out in the previously arranged manner, Sam rushed forward to buy a cure for his bad back. Minutes later he was followed by Thady, seeking a cure for failing eyesight.

Sales went well. Many people seemed convinced by the rhetoric. Sam and Thady were impressed as they saw so much money changing hands.

'Told you the old varmint was rich,' hissed Thady in Sam's ear. 'He makes a goddamned fortune at this!'

Sam hardly heard the remark. His eyes were on Julia as she handed out medicines and took in dollar bills, which she did with practised ease, disguising the stiffness of her arm so that no one noticed it. He was astonished at the change in her. Her face lit up in smiles as she spoke to the customers. She laughed from time to time at their poor jokes. It was as if her whole personality had altered. He knew it was false, just part of the show, but he was happy to see her smile and felt his heart lifting at the sight of her. She made an impression on the crowd, especially with the young men. Obviously, she was a great help to Karl in his business.

At the start, almost as soon as he had begun, Karl had introduced her as a Red Indian princess, possibly a descendant of the legendary Pocahontas. He had thought hard before making such an absurd claim. Folk in some parts of the country were not so dumb but he reckoned the citizens of Fairmount probably were.

Sam's eyes never left Julia for several minutes. There was a feeling growing inside him, which he had not experienced before. How beautiful she was with her winning smile and graceful movement. Then he saw the smile fade to be replaced by shock, then something that he recognized as fear. Her glance dropped to the ground. She seemed to shrink into herself. For a second, she seemed paralysed, then her head lifted and she stared at a point in the crowd with anger and hatred and a suggestion of deep bitterness. In a moment, however, all that was gone, and she smiled at her next customer and made a remark that set the woman laughing.

Sam turned his head towards the place where Julia had been staring. There was a man there, dressed in black, thin, with a hooked nose and tight lips. He was grinning in a way that held no humour but instead cruelty and contempt. As Sam looked, he turned on his heel and pushed his way through the crowd. Then he was sauntering over the square and in a moment had mounted a bay horse and was riding, without a backward look, out of the town. There was a gun at his hip and a rifle at his saddle bow.

Sam stared after him and then back at Julia. She was as before, carrying on with her work as if nothing had happened. He felt a deep anger in the knowledge that she had been, in some way, frightened by the stranger.

In that moment, he resolved to find out what it was that had caused her such fear and to destroy it as best he could.

3

Karl decided to leave Fairmount that same afternoon, as soon as he had picked up some fresh supplies from the store. As he said, he never stayed in the one place more than a couple of days because there were always people likely to come back and pester him about cures that did not seem to be working in spite of his argument that they needed to have patience and give the medicine a little time.

They made pretty good progress and before sundown found themselves a long way from the town. Karl and Julia changed into their normal clothes while Sam and Thady built a fire by the side of the trail and began to heat up the stew which the storekeeper's wife had sold to the party. It promised to be a fine treat on stomachs that had been too used to simpler fare and Sam was pleased at the prospect in spite of the worry that had been in his mind ever since the incident with the stranger. Thady was in a different kind of mood. Out of earshot of their two companions, he grumbled about Karl's seeming determination to go in a direction other than Red Lance.

'Old beaver says we're turning east soon. Some townships he's been to before years ago. Thinks he kin do all right — probably will too! He's a cunning old varmint and no mistake. Knows how to swindle money out of folks with his coloured water and bogus plasters!'

'Some of his stuff may be of help to people. I reckon he knows somethin' about cures and suchlike,' put in Sam defensively, his heart full of sympathy for Julia.

'Knows how to cure himself of being short of cash, I'd say,' snorted Thady. 'Wonder where he keeps it all? In one of them crates in the wagon, I bet!'

'Forget it!' snapped Sam.

36

'You're gittin' soft, ain't ya?' Thady's twitch was worse than ever. 'We'll never git to Lewis by pussy-footing around like this! It would be easy! We kin take them both by surprise. Don't need to do them any harm. Jest take the money and the horses and go — *and* the guns. We'll need them.'

'You'll do it without me,' answered Sam steadily. 'In fact, against me. I told you them folks has helped us real good and we can't turn on them as if we were a couple of vipers.'

'All the time I've known you, I never thought you had much of a conscience. Now you're gittin' like a school-marm! That girl got something to do with it?'

'Maybe . . . but I wouldn't do it to the old man either. Put it all out of your mind, Thady!'

They were joined just then by the other two and they all sat down to eat. Karl rattled on at great length about his successful day of business but was careful not to mention how much money he had made. Thady supped his stew morosely and made a poor attempt to conceal his dissatisfaction. Sam watched the girl, who ate in silence, and stared into the fire, answering only briefly when Karl spoke to her. In the firelight, and sitting close together, they did not look alike at all. There was no trace of a family resemblance and he came to the conclusion that they were not related. This was not Karl's daughter, as he had claimed. Thady was right about that. So, what had brought them together?

He could not guess, any more than he could guess at the reason for her fear when she saw the ferrety-looking guy in the square. In his heart, Sam wanted very much to help her but there seemed no way.

The thought troubled him all night as he lay under the wagon, as usual, alongside Thady. Overhead, he could hear the old man snoring but there was no sound from Julia. In spite of her not being his daughter, they sure acted as if she were. They were natural with one another just as if they were family. But there was nothing wrong about it. He felt sure of that.

In the morning they were up early, preparing to move off. Thady was clearing away the breakfast gear while Sam attached the team to the wagon. Karl walked over to Sam as if to converse in a casual way.

'You fellers have been some help to me over the last few days but I may as well let you know straight that we'll be parting company tomorrow. Thing is, I have a friend not so far from here who can help out and I'll get him to join us. You were good enough at the sale — especially for beginners — but this old buddy of mine is a lot better. He has the technique of gittin' the crowd real excited and eager to buy. He's also a pretty good teamster. So, I'll be taking him on. I'll pay you guys what you deserve and wish you luck on your way.'

He paused as if expecting some reply from Sam but there was none. Surprise had changed to dismay at the thought of leaving Julia.

'May as well tell you another thing,' went on Karl. 'You seem an all-right kid to me but your partner there ain't quite so clear-cut. Jumpy guys like him, I don't trust. I'd just as soon not have him around. He's got some kind of a gripe which is going to lead to trouble. Maybe you should think about that yourself and try to find different company and a new life. I know it ain't my business but I've been around a long time and seen it all. Thanks for having respect for my daughter. You always spoke to her polite.'

He sauntered off as if he had been talking about the weather and left Sam to inform Thady of the change in plan. Sam stood thoughfully looking after Karl's retreating figure. Somehow, he did not really believe the story of the old friend mentioned by Karl. It seemed to him that Thady was not trusted by either Karl or Julia and they wanted rid of him. It meant losing Sam too in the circumstances but there was no help for that. Also, it was as if these two, Karl and Julia, were so used to being together, just by themselves, that there was no room for others. The thought brought a tinge of jealousy into his mind which he thrust aside.

'That's it,' growled Thady, when he heard the news. 'I ain't leaving without a good handful of them dollars. Believe me — '

'Don't push your luck!' rapped Sam, in anger. 'He's all ready for you anyway. That gun's still at his belt and I don't think he would be slow to use it.'

They made off not much later with Sam at the reins and Thady sitting gloomily beside him. There was no conversation and Sam did not attempt any. His feelings about Thady were changing. He felt only a rising anxiety that there would be none of the trouble hinted at by Karl.

Later, somewhere around midday, Thady was called into the wagon and told to get some rest. To Sam's surprise, the old man stayed there as well and the girl came out to sit beside him. He guessed it was her idea and he felt much flattered.

They did not speak much. Sam tried a few remarks about the team and the wagon and the townships up ahead but it was all flat and empty talk. What he really wanted to say was that he thought she was beautiful and was distressed at the prospect of leaving her. But there was no chance of expressing himself in any such way. It was all made worse by the fact that she smiled at him now as if she really liked him, in spite of the unease at the back of her eyes which had to do with the man in the square.

He could not speak about that either, although he seethed with anger whenever he thought of the guy.

Later, Karl took Sam's place and the wagon travelled on for some miles further with all conversation halted. Every person on board was busy with private thoughts. Karl recognized the mood of Julia and knew how she was feeling. He had spoken much about business in an enthusiastic way the evening before but his mind had been on the stranger. She had told him of the dark-clothed man in the crowd who had looked at her in such a sinister way. She did not remember the man but knew he was from her past life and represented danger. Karl understood. He had not seen the man but guessed where he fitted into Julia's life and his own. He wondered if the past would re-emerge or drift away. There was nothing to be said, however, in the presence of Sam and Thady.

Sam sat in the shade of the wagon canvas with his heart full of trouble. He found it hard to face the knowledge that he must soon be parted from Julia. He guessed she had sat beside him on the buckboard to make it plain that she was no longer suspicious of him and, in fact, had a liking for him. He knew it was not a feeling she had for Thady whom she still looked at like a dog she suspected of carrying rabies. It wasn't exactly fair, thought Sam, as he glanced over at his dozing partner. Thady hadn't done anything bad to them — not yet at any rate — nor would he . . .

He reckoned maybe he had fallen asleep in the heat when he was awakened by the wagon coming to a stop. A voice drifted in through the gap in the canvas just behind the buckboard. He did not take in the words but he recognized the tone of threat which the voice carried.

He eased himself into a kneeling position, at the same time, motioning Thady to remain quiet. From the dark of the interior he could make out the figure of a horseman in the bright sunlight outside. He peered carefully and caught his breath as he recognized the man in the black jacket who had so upset Julia the day before. There came a slight movement of the bay horse and Sam saw a Colt .44 in the man's hand. It was pointed steadily at Karl.

'Jest keep your hands on the reins,

Doctor Swigg-Hardy,' the chuckle was sarcastic, 'or I'll blow all your brains — if you have any — all over that little Injun princess. I ain't too fussy how this goes. It don't matter whether you hand over the money alive or I take it when you're dead.'

Sam tensed and then felt his whole body tremble. He could see Julia's back and her right arm, rigid with dread.

'Swigg-Hardy, heh, heh, that's pretty good!' the voice went on. 'Gunslinger turns bottle-swinger, eh? Killing them with pills now instead of bullets! What do you call that little bitch beside you? Injun princess! You've got to be kidding! It's been a long time, sure, but I remember her. She's growed into a fine-lookin' gal. Her mother was a real dream, as I remember. Prettiest little Mexican woman me and the boys ever came across. She shouldn't have put up such a fight, though. Pete jest lost his temper in the end and knifed her. You remember that, don't you, kid? If it hadn't been for Karl here, you would likely have gone the same way. Some of the boys had a fancy, even for you!'

The man fell silent. Sam could hear Julia's sharp breath but she remained motionless, as did Karl. The gun remained trained on the old man. Sam knew the outlaw was quite unaware of the presence of Thady and himself. He could have had no idea that anyone else was with Karl and Julia when the two younger men were mixing in with the crowd yesterday. Sam's mind raced as he tried to figure out what to do. Then he saw the butt of the rifle lying in the shade of the canvas where Julia had placed it. He eased himself forward and stretched out a hand. He did not dare to breathe as he gripped the wood and drew it towards him. It made a slight sound on the board but this was drowned by movement from the restless team outside.

'What the hell did you shoot Pete for?' went on the voice, not as a serious question, but in a spirit of sarcasm. 'Condor and Pete and the rest of us were only having fun! You gunned down Condor too. You realize that? He ain't never forgot it! Lucky for you that you got to that horse so quick. Looks like your luck has jest about run out today, though, wouldn't you say?'

Sam covered the safety catch of the rifle with his arm as he slipped it off, praying that the sound would not carry. He raised the rifle. He had not fired a gun for many years but there was no time to practise. He could see the man's eyes. The jeering light had gone out of them. In its place came the death sentence, cold and without pity. There was a new message there too — it was about killing the old man and then doing what he liked with the girl . . .

Sam steadied his whole body and aimed at the black waistcoat. He breathed out slowly and at the same time pulled the trigger, easy and without jerking . . .

Even so, he was surprised at the recoil. The rifle jumped in his hands and the bullet struck, not into the black waistcoat, but into the throat above the red bandanna.

Blood rushed in a mighty torrent. There came a strangled scream and the man swayed in the saddle and then toppled over backwards as his horse leaped to one side. His body hit the ground with a thump. There he lay, jerking wildly while blood pumped from his throat and mouth and spread over jacket and shirt and face and began to soak into the parched earth.

They remained transfixed until the wild death throes ceased. Then Karl stepped carefully down and walked over to the dead man. His gun was in his hand now but pointed idly to the ground. He gazed at the bloody corpse and then back to the wagon where Sam had appeared on the buckboard, rifle still in his hands.

'Good boy.' The old man's voice was scarcely above a whisper, while his eyes gleamed in gratitude and admiration. 'Good boy . . . '

A small hand gripped Sam's arm.

Julia was shivering, her face pale, eyes brimming with tears. He patted her on the shoulder, not knowing what else to do, placed the rifle carefully on the boards and then stepped to the ground. There, he almost fell over. His whole body trembled and he held on to the wagon for support. Then he straightened up and walked to where Karl stood over the corpse.

It was a hideous mess; face contorted in fear and pain and half-covered in blood, clothing disturbed and blood-soaked. He stared, realizing he had never killed a man before. He had thought of it often and had seen himself, in his imagination, shoot Lewis a thousand times. This seemed quite different. It was an irrevocable act, justified, sure, in these circumstances, but something that could never be changed and never be cancelled out.

As a boy, he had sometimes gone hunting, generally shooting jack-rabbits or a deer for the pot. One day he had shot a bear and had stood over it, staring at the fine animal, lying with blood in its mouth, and he had felt like a louse because he had killed it for no reason. That guilt had remained with him for a long time. Even in prison, he had sometimes dreamed of it.

He felt, nevertheless, that this must be different. There had been good reason . . . Julia and Karl and maybe Thady and himself — they were the reason.

'You saved our lives, Sam,' Karl's hand was on his shoulder, 'I'll not forget it.'

Sam resisted the impulse to say something trite like 'It's OK', and also put out of his mind the idea of asking Karl anything about the man. He had come to realize there were matters Karl and Julia did not talk about to anyone else. Still, he had heard enough to make looking at the corpse easier and dispel any sense of guilt or remorse.

'I guess we'd better try to find a sheriff,' grunted Sam, stating what seemed obvious to him, although the notion of what that would involve turned his stomach.

Karl did not answer for a long moment, then he kicked the body slightly with the toe of his boot, not with malice but as if deep in thought.

'Well, that's the usual thing, sure enough,' he said, voice careful and controlled, 'but this here business ain't all that straightforward. For one thing, you and your buddy are just out of jail. That means whatever you say ain't likely to be believed. Guys like you are put in prison as a punishment for what you did — whatever that was — and I ain't never asked you — and when you git out, you're expected to go straight and make an honest life for yourself, but it ain't made easy because nobody trusts you or what you say.'

'Yeah, well, that's true enough, as it seems to me,' answered Sam. 'But there's you and Julia. You saw it all.'

'I know it but when I was a younger man, me and the law didn't always see eye to eye either. I've got a lot more to argue about than the likes of this feller. There are old sheriffs and marshals in some parts who would reach for their guns if they read about me in the newspapers, so I ain't chancing it.'

He glanced at them, noting their surprise, and then turned away. What he had said was the truth. These old lawmen would not hesitate to do everything possible to bring him in, not just because of the crimes he had committed, but because he had been one of their own, a lawman himself, before he had been fool enough to throw all that away by keeping stolen money that ought to have been returned to its rightful owners. In the eyes of the law there could be no greater crime than such a betrayal and, in the depths of his soul, he agreed and had spent many a restless night cursing the foolhardiness of his youth which had given way to temptation and made him an outlaw.

The stolen money had soon been wasted and he had drifted out West, all those years ago, to make what kind of a living he could, poking cattle or labouring on the farms. It had been rough and he had slipped once again into crime. There had been many a challenge from men as wild as himself. Always he had met such challenges head on, gun to gun, never a bullet in the back, but against the law, nevertheless.

It was about that time he had met Condor, that slippery eel of a man, always out for himself. He had been handy with a gun too but they had never fallen out seriously enough to stand face to face, with fingers itching on triggers.

That was, until the terrible day, years after they had lost sight of one another, when Karl had heard the Mexican woman scream and had gone in with guns blazing. Condor had gone down in the savage fight but Karl, with the girl to save and the gang surrounding him, had not stopped to see if he had survived. Somehow, though, he had never really believed the shot had been fatal.

Karl shook his head, trying to rid himself of memories that tormented him. It was all a long time ago. Since then, he had led a peaceful life with this crazy snake-oil man set-up, which was legal, if not quite straight. His guns had long cooled and he had looked after the girl as if he were her father.

Now, though, things were changing. As he had waited for death on the buckboard, he had looked into the eyes of the man with the gun and had known that when the name of Condor was uttered it was not to refer to a man who was dead or very far away.

He would face Condor again soon. He felt sure of that . . .

4

Sam and Thady took turns with the spade from the wagon as they dug the grave a few yards from the trail. The ground was hard and the heat from the sun overpowering and soon Thady was in a sweat.

'Be as well to leave the feller to the wolves and coyotes,' he spat, 'as wear ourselves out with this!'

'Always cover your tracks,' answered Sam wisely.

'You're beginning to sound like that old buzzard over there,' growled Thady, with little humour. 'He seems to think he knows everything too.'

At last they had dug a hole deep enough for the job and returned to pick up the corpse. Karl was standing by the body with the gunbelt and a few other things in his hands.

'Here's a wallet and a fine gold watch

and about twenty dollars,' he stated. 'All of this belongs rightly to you, Sam, and the horse and saddle and rifle too. If it wasn't for you, we'd be lying here dead in the dirt with this vulture grinning over us.'

'Well, I don't know,' answered Sam. 'It don't seem right.'

'Sounds all right to me,' objected Thady. 'Jest what we need.'

Thady was scowling as they carried the corpse to the grave and tumbled it in without ceremony, before covering it with dirt and stones.

'What the hell do ya mean?' he grumbled. 'We need a horse and the guns and the money too! No sense in saying that it don't seem right to take the guy's gear after you've killed him, is there? Use your head, Sam!'

When they got back to Karl, Sam agreed to take the dead man's property if there was no feeling about it and Karl and Julia did not need any of it for themselves.

'It's all yours,' said Karl. 'Nobody

else has any right to it.' He still had the wallet in his hand and drew out a small slip of paper. 'This here's a pay-check. Name of Starlight Mining Company.' He glanced at Thady as he spoke. 'Made out to Joe Maxwell. I guess that was him. Don't seem any kind of a miner to me. Clothes too fancy and hands soft. More like a gunslinger, if you ask me.'

He paused, remembering that terrible fight long ago, but resolving to keep his mouth shut about that. It was to do with Julia and himself only. He did not know how much of the gunman's talk had been overheard by Sam and Thady but felt it was not much. Anyway, he had no intention of adding to it.

Sam was looking at his face, guessing at his thoughts. He had heard enough of what was said at the buckboard to tell him that Karl had saved Julia from a gang of drunken ruffians on the day her mother was murdered. He knew, also, that it was not a subject to be discussed. Karl had not referred to it so there was nothing further to be said. He did not think Thady had heard much, if anything, and decided to tell him nothing. Thady seemed to be getting queerer in the head and might well alarm or hurt Julia by speaking out of turn.

'Here, take this.' Karl had thrust the gun and other objects into Sam's hands. Thady snatched the pay-check to have a closer look. He read the name of the mine-owner, Thomas Lewis, printed upon it. He gasped involuntarily, nostrils widening like a hound dog on a close scent, but said nothing. Nevertheless, Karl observed his reaction but remained impassive.

'Reckon I'll go and make sure thet bay doesn't wander off,' grunted Thady.

He went to attend to the horse. Sam was looking over at the wagon where Julia sat motionless.

'She all right?' he asked anxiously.

'Bit shocked,' answered Karl.

'I would like her to have this watch,' offered Sam.

'She won't want anything that belonged to that rattler,' said Karl, shaking his head.

Sam knew why. It wasn't just what had happened today.

'You take it then, Karl. It isn't much use to me I ain't counting the day in minutes.'

'You fellers still going to Red Lance?' asked Karl suddenly. He watched Sam nod his head and then pursed his lips. 'OK, it's up to you. I guess you're still both buddies with your own plans, but remember what I said about your sidekick. He needs to be kept an eye on. Here's something to add to the twenty dollars. It's your pay and a bonus for doing what you did with my old rifle.' He thrust a wad of bills in to Sam's hand. 'Now, since you're determined to make for Red Lance, the way to do it is to follow this trail for about ten miles and then turn off on the track heading west. After a while you'll come to a place belonging to a feller called Jason. He'll sell you a horse but don't give him more than half the price he first asks for. Go easy on the bay. One horse and two riders ain't never fair to the horse.'

Sam thanked him and then walked slowly towards the wagon. He saw Julia stiffen slightly as he approached her. For a moment, he did not know what to say, then he told her that he and Thady were going.

'I feel real sorry about it,' he added, summoning up his courage. 'Thing is — I hope you don't mind me saying this — I've got to be real fond of you.'

'It's kind of you to say so,' she replied, a slight tremble in her voice. 'Thank you so much for what you did. We'll never forget it.'

That was all. It seemed to him that a million things remained unsaid. He turned away with some sense of despair and walked over to where Thady and Karl stood with the horse.

'Time to get going,' grinned Thady,

'if you've finished your goodbyes.'

Karl frowned, shook off his irritation, and then looked at the ground where a bloodstain about the length of a man's forearm caught his eye. He began to kick dirt over it with the toe of his boot. Then he looked steadily at Sam. Something of his old lawman's way of thinking was coming back to him.

'You need to think a bit about what it's going to be like riding into Red Lance on Joe Maxwell's horse. A man's horse gets to be as familiar as himself to folks round about. If you're determined to get to the mine to ask fer work, that just makes it all the more likely that it will be recognized. Take my advice and exchange it for another horse when you git to Jason's place. He'll be quite willing if he thinks he's getting a good deal.'

Sam and Thady nodded agreement and then rode away with Thady sitting behind Sam on the bay. They glanced back to see Karl looking at the watch in his hand and then turn towards the wagon. Sam sighed and rode on a little faster. After some miles, however, he insisted they dismount and walk to save overstraining the animal.

'Well, I guess it's your horse so there ain't no argument,' said Thady. 'Come to think of it, though, when do I git my two bits from all that money the old muskrat gave you? I know you're sure the blue-eyed boy with them two but I got a right to some pay as well!'

He brightened up when he saw there was more than enough to buy an extra horse and patted the rifle which hung at the saddle bow.

'We'll git even with that Lewis skunk yet, believe me!' he vowed.

He kept on with the same refrain for much of the day and continued when they felt the need to rest as darkness fell. He even attempted to read the old newspaper report again while he supped his coffee but gave up and dropped off to sleep, still grumbling. Sam stared at the night sky, feeling much troubled, his heart heavy from his parting with Julia and apprehensive of the future.

'You ever killed anybody before?' asked Sam over their meagre breakfast, next day.

'Ain't sure. Got into a gunfight once with some guys up near Bullhead River. Hit some of them.'

'They die?'

'Don't know. I didn't stick around long enough to find out.'

'How do you feel about that? I mean if you reckoned they might have been killed?'

'Feel? Nothin'. What the hell do you mean? You feeling all right yourself, this morning?'

Sam felt maybe Thady was right. Men carried guns in this part of the world in expectation of having to use them. There was no use in worrying too much about the consequences. Maxwell had deserved all he got, anyway, and there was still Lewis to deal with. He had no intention of backing out of that any more than had Thady. Still, he hoped that might be the end of it.

Sometime in the afternoon they came in sight of the Jason place. It wasn't much to look at, just a couple of rough-looking shacks and a paddock with two horses. Jason was standing at the gate as they approached. He was of short stature and heavily built with a balding head which showed up when he took off his hat to scratch. He had lost half of his left ear and there was an ugly scar on his cheek.

'Howdy!' he called out, waving a hand. 'You fellers jest passing through, or what?'

'Here on business,' answered Sam from the saddle. He did not like the look of Jason but had made up his mind to be as pleasant as possible so as to get the purchase of the horses settled with all speed. 'Mr Plinston directed us here. Says you deal in horseflesh.'

'Yeah, live mostly!' The grin did not reach Jason's eyes. 'Plinston, eh, Karl Plinston? Well, well, come on in! I've done business with Karl before. You're welcome. Time for coffee!'

He led the bay through the gate and up to the shack and watched closely as Sam dismounted. Thady, who had been walking alongside for about an hour, looked pleased at the prospect of coffee. Sam was not quite so keen but there seemed no point in risking offence to the horse-dealer.

They went into the shack while an Indian youth took the horse. The place looked just as bad inside as it did on the outside. There were a few pieces of unpainted furniture and a dirty-looking bed in the corner. On one wall stood an unlit stove with a cold coffee pot on top. Jason motioned them to sit down.

'Tell me about old Karl.' He smiled sloppily. 'He still doing that snake-oil man stunt?'

'Sure,' answered Thady. 'Doing all right too!'

'I bet! Pretty smart feller that Karl! How about that cute little piece of honeysuckle? He still playing the big bumble-bee with her?'

'Nope!' snapped Sam. 'No bumble-bee, jest a fine girl and a decent man. Anyhow, we came here to talk business and we don't have much time.'

Jason scowled. He looked straight at Sam, a glimmer of hostility half-hidden behind his eyelids.

'Sure, sure, let's hurry on with the business,' he growled. 'What do you have in mind?'

'We need a horse — well, two horses . . . '

'Two?'

'We was thinking of exchanging the bay for something else and buying another.'

'Somethin' wrong with the bay?'

'Nope, we jest could do with a change,' answered Sam unconvincingly, but in a tone that brooked no argument.

Jason nodded to himself, a faint smile at the corner of his mouth.

'All right. What happened to the other horse? Drop dead on you?'

'Yeah, that's it,' said Thady.

'You bring the saddle and all the rest?'

'We couldn't carry everything, for Christ's sake!' snapped Thady, giving up on the coffee.

'Well, all that stuff costs money — about as much as a horse. It will cost you. Still, I suppose you have it — the money, I mean . . .'

He rose from the chair as they both nodded and led them from the shack out to the corral. It contained only the two horses they had already seen from the gate. They both looked hungry and neglected and one was lame.

'This it? Well, we'll have to keep the bay after all and buy the roan,' decided Sam.

'The one with four legs,' agreed Thady.

Jason was looking at the gun in Sam's belt, then he glanced over at the bay, standing with the Indian youth. He seemed to be deep in thought for a moment before he named his price.

Mindful of Karl's warning, Sam suggested half the stated amount for the horse and about two thirds for the saddle and harness. To his surprise, Jason did not haggle.

'Fine, fine,' he said. 'Now let's have that drink while the Choctaw gits the critter ready.'

Back in the shack, the money was paid over and Jason shoved two dirty-looking glasses in front of them and poured out whiskey. He poured another for himself, grinning now as if in a good humour. Thady drank gratefully but Sam took a sip only.

'Where are you fellers heading, then?'

Thady told him about Red Lance and the idea of finding work at the mine.

'That so? You guys in silver-mining? I kind of thought maybe you were. That's Mr Lewis's place. Likely enough he could do with some young hands. I'll give you directions about the quickest way of reaching Red

Lance. It's a pretty long ride but you'll get there. You know Mr Lewis?'

'Nope.'

'Fine man. You'll be all right with him. Too bad you can't stay longer for another drink. Next time you see Karl, give him my regards.' Jason looked straight at Sam. 'That girl, prettiest little filly I ever did see. Too bad you never got to know her better . . . '

He stopped as he saw Sam's fist clench but twisted his mouth in a little grin, pleased to have needled this young feller who was obviously soft on Karl's cute little bunny. That Karl, he thought again, hell of a guy . . .

A few minutes later, Sam and Thady rode out on the bay and the roan, while Jason waved them goodbye and the Indian lad looked on. Thady was in good spirits and was talking about getting even with Lewis almost before they were out of earshot.

Jason watched them go, a sardonic grin creeping over his heavy features. Who did these guys think they were kidding? Miners? A couple of ex-cons if ever he saw any — and with Joe Maxwell's horse and gun too!

Joe had called into Jason's place only about a week before because the bay was losing a shoe. The Indian had fixed it, while Joe had drunk whiskey and told Jason that he worked at Starlight as foreman. Now there came riding in two dead-beats with Joe's horse and gun and money and full of lies and bull about looking for work. Murder and robbery — that was for sure! Clear as daylight! Trying to rid themselves of Joe's horse too in case somebody recognized it . . . Well, somebody *had* — himself — and he was going to fix them good.

For a moment, he wondered how to handle it. He could send a message by the Indian boy to the sheriff at Sweetholm but there was nothing much in that for himself. He believed a meeting with an important man like Thomas Lewis, the owner of the Starlight silver mine, could be of great advantage to him. Business opportunities might well arise from it. At least, a useful acquaintanceship would be created — possibly even a friendship — and Jason felt sure that Lewis would show his gratitude at once with a generous financial reward.

There was a way to reach the mine in much less time than the forty-mile journey facing the two ex-cons on their way to Red Lance. It involved a ride through the rugged hills to the west, which was hard going, and part of it would have to be made at night. It could be done with the help of the Choctaw acting as guide but they would need to start without delay.

The prospect did not appeal to Jason. He was not a man who liked to exert himself if it could be avoided and this journey seemed formidable. When he thought, however, of the riches which Lewis must possess, he was convinced he should make the effort.

'Hey, Choctaw!' he called harshly. 'Saddle up my white and git your own horse ready! We got some riding to do!'

He returned to the shack for his rifle and to pack some small amount of food for the long night ahead.

5

Lewis was up before the sun rose over the tree-lined hill to the east. He always slept badly as the pain in his back and legs gnawed into his mind and set him grunting and turning over and over a thousand times until he was driven to rise before light came into the sky.

Still dressed in his night robe, he had dragged himself from bed and hobbled on his two sticks to the chair by the window. The woman who kept house for him heard his movements as always and appeared with hot, sweet coffee which he sipped gratefully as he attempted to move his limbs into a position that held less pain.

His hair, once jet-black, had whitened and there were lines in his face which made him look older than his years. He did not believe he could live very much longer and something in his heart told him he did not want to. He was rich, sure, and he had a fine house and a carriage to use when he had to travel. He had a couple of servants and there were many men working for him in the mine which had brought him the riches he had long desired, but his crippled condition seemed to him to cancel it all out. There was a bitterness within him which was as ever-present as his pain.

As usual, he looked that morning over the mine buildings spread out in the narrow valley below and drew what comfort he could from their existence. The place was still doing all right — not so well as in the past, but pretty good.

He was snapped out of his reverie by the sudden appearance of three horsemen climbing slowly up the steep path to his house. The man in front he recognized at once as one of the guards whom he always had spread out around his property. The other two lagged further behind and he made out details of them only by degrees as they approached. There was a heavy-looking man in a wide hat and a youth who seemed to be an Indian to judge by the way he rode and his shoulder-length hair. The trio rode around the house and after the sound of voices came the sound of his personal bodyguard knocking at the door.

'Somebody to see you, Mr Lewis, feller calls himself Jason.'

Lewis turned in his seat and at the same time drew open the desk drawer in which he kept a handgun. He had never heard of Jason and it seemed queer to have visitors at such an early hour.

'All right,' he said. 'Bring him in.'

Jason did not look impressive. His heavy face was heavier than ever with fatigue. There was sweat on his forehead and he was breathing in gasps as if he had walked up the hill instead of astride his horse. He also smelled badly enough to make Lewis push his chair back a little way nearer the window.

After he had regained his breath, Jason told the story of the two jailbirds who had come to his place with Joe Maxwell's horse and gun and who claimed they were making for Red Lance. He had stolen a march on them, of course, so they would not be there yet and Mr Lewis had time to deal with them in any way he wanted.

Lewis kept his anger in check when he heard about Joe, who had worked for him for years. Joe was in what was known as 'administration' at Starlight. In other words, Lewis employed him and several others in activities which were far from legal but which brought in a good profit. The proceeds of bank robberies and holdups were easily concealed in a business such as silver mining and no one suspected an upstanding citizen like Mr Thomas Lewis. Maxwell had always been invaluable. Was it really possible that he had been killed?

Lewis rarely allowed his feelings to show in his face and, to start with, he was not too sure if he could trust Jason to be telling the truth, although there seemed no reason why the man should come here with such a tall tale if there was no truth in it.

'These guys say why they were coming to Red Lance?' he asked at last.

'They said they were lookin' for work in your mine, Mr Lewis,' smirked Jason. 'Seems jest like lies to me. These guys ain't no miners.'

'How do you know they're jest out of jail?'

'Haircuts. Look as if they'd been near scalped. Dead give-away to a man like me who keeps his eyes open.'

'Yeah, you've kept your eyes open, sure enough . . . '

Lewis thought carefully about what had been said. Joe could have fallen foul of a couple of dead-beats returning to a life of crime as soon as they got out of prison. Something about it was beginning to strike a chord in the back of his mind. Two guys in jail, both released at the same time and sticking together . . . ?

'These fellers give you their names?'

'Thady and Sam — that's what they called each other.'

'Jesus Christ!' For a moment Lewis forgot to keep a tight rein on his tongue. It was all flooding back. Those two hicks he had made use of in robbing that little bank all that time ago! They had been sentenced to jail, when was it — ten or twelve years past? He remembered reading about it in the newspapers not long before he used the stolen money to make his first venture into the silver-mining business — a venture which had been crowned with such success. He had been surprised to learn they had escaped the gallows but that had been explained in the newspapers. Could it really be them? Who else could it be? Jason wasn't making these names up! So they were out and searching for this mine, which meant they were looking for him. There could only be one reason

— they were out for revenge.

Jason was staring at him . . . 'You know these guys, Mr Lewis?'

'No, no, I'm jest blazing mad at what they've done. It's certain they've killed Joe. My foreman, murdered by a couple of criminals jest out of prison!'

'You could set the law on them if you wanted. I was thinking about bringing in the sheriff from Sweetholm but I reckoned you would want to deal with it yourself, Mr Lewis. That's why I came over all this way in the middle of the night. I'm sure tired out, I can tell you!'

'Yeah, and I'm grateful. I'll see you get well rewarded and I'll deal with these two, believe me! Whether I'll bring in the law or not, I ain't made up my mind yet.'

That was not true. He *had* made up his mind to leave the law out of it. These two stinking hicks might have too much to say about the past if they were arrested. Even if they were not believed, a suspicion might be left, and

Lewis wanted above all things to maintain his reputation in the eyes of the law. He had enough men and guns up here to fix a couple of muskrats who had come back to stick their noses into his life. He would settle them once and for all. He found it hard to credit, just the same, that they had killed Joe, one of the best men he had.

'Did they give any kind of clue about where this might have happened — with Joe, I mean? Where they were before they came to you? Did they say exactly?'

'Not exactly. They said they was with Karl Plinston. I think they were travelling around together for two or three days.'

'Karl who?'

'Plinston.'

'Who the hell's Karl Plinston?'

'Snake-oil man. One of them travelling doctors. Goes around with a wagon selling stuff that's supposed to cure folks of all the goddamned ailments that he kin think up.' Jason grinned with amusement for the first time. 'Hell of a guy, really. Has this half-Mexican girl with him. Jest a filly to tell you the truth, not much more than a kid, but as pretty as a rosebud in a churchyard. Kind of girl that kin send a man half crazy jest by looking at him, only she looks cold all the time, like as if she was telling you to keep your distance, or else.'

Lewis straightened himself in his chair, sending a sudden pain shooting up his back.

'Mexican-looking girl, you say . . . anything else about her?'

'Has a stiff arm. Must have hurt it somehow. It don't detract much from her looks, though, I kin tell you.'

Lewis did not move at all. He sat as if deep in thought, while Jason stared at him in surprise. When he eventually spoke, his voice had changed. It had become charged with barely controlled excitement.

'This feller, Karl whatsisname, about what age is he, do you reckon?'

'Well, maybe sixty, somethin' like that. Still tough as hell, though, I would say . . . '

'His face . . . What's his face like, for Christ's sake?'

'What? Well, kind of big nose, eyes sharp like a ferret, some kind of little scar over his right eye.'

'He carry a gun?'

'Yeah, always when I've seen him. It bulges under his coat.'

'Which side?'

'Left.'

'He left-handed, this guy?'

'Yeah, I guess so. Come to think of it, he always — '

'All right. Where do you think he's heading?'

'Can't rightly say. These guys didn't tell me. He must have been down the trail near Catjump Ridge, though, when I think of the way they came.'

'OK. Tell you what, Mr Jason, you've been a great help, telling me all this. I'll take care of them two coyotes, don't worry about that, and I'll make sure you're well compensated for all your trouble. If you ever see anything else that might be interesting, I hope you'll let me know. Now, I got work to do, so you get to the kitchen where my woman will fix you up with somethin' to eat and you kin catch up on your sleep before you go back home. Thanks a million fer what you've done.'

Jason, being dismissed more abruptly than he had bargained for, went off as instructed, his face showing dejection and some puzzlement at the turn in the conversation.

Lewis twisted a little in his chair and looked out of the window. The sun was now well up and the heat of the day could already be felt. Against the blue sky a hawk hovered and swooped down a short distance and then rose to hover again. There were sounds beginning to rise from the mine — men's voices shouting and the din of a hammer against metal. Lewis's eyes saw the hawk but his brain did not; his ears heard the hammer but his brain did not register it. All he could see was Karl Pochard, as he had called himself, young and dark, and swift with his left-hand draw and all he heard was the thunder of the Colt .45 as men who had foolishly challenged Karl leaped with the shock of the bullet and dropped like felled cattle to the ground.

That had been many years ago when the reputation of the left-handed gunslinger had been known as far north as Des Moines. Lewis, known at that time as Condor, had seen him then once or twice and, knowing his reputation, had avoided looking too closely into those cold, grey eyes.

Later, very much later, just after Lewis had struck a rich vein of silver, there had been another meeting. This time the memory was like a splash of blood to the brain. Lewis and some of his men had gone out to celebrate. They had gone to Sweetholm because the town held a couple of swell saloons and they had taken a hell of a lot to drink which made Joe and Pete and the rest of them just about crazy. On the way back in the early morning, after a night that none of them could remember, they had met a Mexican woman and her little girl and things had got rapidly out of hand.

The woman had struggled but she was no match for a gang of determined drunks. There had been a lot of coarse laughing and her clothes had been torn off and in the end she had been utterly overpowered, with the little girl screaming in mad hysteria. Pete had lost his head altogether, though, and had knifed the woman, mostly just because that was the kind of guy he was.

Then, seemingly from nowhere, Karl had appeared and that left-handed gun had blazed. Pete's brains had been spattered for yards. Lewis had taken a bullet in his lower back. Joe had his shirt ripped by another. Neil had gone down with the calf of his leg taken right out like the inside of a lemon. It had all been mad, like a kind of nightmare. Lewis remembered writhing in the dirt, cursing at the pain of that red-hot bullet, and seeing Karl pulling the young girl up into the saddle. Shots had still been coming from Kit Williams and Marty Hendrix and the girl had suddenly screamed even louder as if she had just been hit. Then they had gone as Karl had ridden like hell into the trees.

Since then Karl had not been heard of. It was as if he had disappeared into thin air. But now he seemed to have returned to the margins of Lewis's life, the life which was like daily torture as the inoperable injury on the edges of his spine worsened from year to year and he had gone from being a wounded man limping around the mine complex to a helpless cripple, unable to move far unaided.

He did not believe he was likely to live much longer but he would die happier if he knew Karl had gone first.

How to achieve that, though, was the problem. He could send out men to find his old enemy and gun him down when his back was turned. Finding him should be easy if he was still going around with that crazy snake-oil outfit but Lewis did not want to sit here and be told one day that Karl had been finished off. Deep inside, he knew he had to be there. He wanted to see his enemy die. If a way could be found for him to do the shooting himself, it would be perfect.

He smiled at the prospect and smiling was an unusual thing for Lewis. He called to his bodyguard to enter the room.

'Those two Osage, the Injuns who help with the horses, tell them to come here in about an hour and to be ready to hit the trail. I got a scouting job for them.' He hesitated for a moment as if clearing his mind. 'And git Hendrix up here too. Soon as he kin move himself. We got things to discuss.'

While he was waiting for Hendrix, his mind was still racing. Karl would not come if he knew for certain he was walking into a trap. There was little doubt he would want to kill Lewis for what had been done to the woman and the girl and he would have taken his revenge long since if he had ever guessed that his most hated enemy and the owner of the Starlight silver mine were one and the same.

If Karl could be persuaded to come to the mine, then it should be easy. It was necessary to make him drop his guard. For a moment, Lewis considered telling the truth about his physical condition so that it would seem like a walkover, but immediately rejected the idea. Karl would not move against a crippled man. It was not his way. He had to think it would be face to face, gun to gun, like the old days, not an easy victory over a sick man but not a bear-trap either. Some element of doubt needed to be sown — something that might just pull him in . . .

Lewis thought for some minutes and then wrote in the tidy hand he had cultivated since the change in his fortunes:

Karl,

I hear you are moving around in a wagon not so far from here, which is Starlight silver mine, near Red Lance. I am the owner of the place and I am a rich man, not like in the old days, when I only had a gun to help me make a living. You were like that too, at that time, but now I hear from your two friends, Thady and Sam, that you sell medicines. These two fellers are with me now. They had a bit of a grudge about something that happened a long time ago but now we've made it up and they are going to work for me.

I know you have a grudge too, about that Mexican woman and what happened when the boys got too much to drink. I've been sorry about that for a long time. I took one of your bullets, which was pretty bad and painful, but now it has healed itself.

If you want to let bygones be

bygones, that's all right by me, and you are welcome to come here. If you are interested, we could maybe go into partnership in the silver business, and it wouldn't cost you a dollar because of the way I feel about the Mex woman.

But if you still have the same old grudge then come anyway or I can meet you somewhere else and we'll have it out, fair and square, gun to gun, and get it settled once and for all.

Let me know through the bearer of this letter,

Thomas Lewis (Condor).

He read it over with a tiny smile on his lips. It wouldn't matter too much whether Karl fell for the friendly slap on the back stuff or wanted to make a duel of it. The result would be about the same.

He licked and stuck the envelope just as Hendrix came into the room.

6

The trail had been rising for several miles and there were many more trees than before. Up ahead, the slopes looked well timbered and there was a sweet scent of resin in the air. Sam breathed in deeply, smiling a little with pleasure in spite of his inner tension.

'Can't be far from Red Lance now,' he remarked. 'If that feller Jason was right about the distance.'

'Yeah, guess you're right,' answered Thady. 'Then we'll git Lewis.'

'We need a plan. We need to figure out how we're going to do this.'

'Well, what the hell, like we always said. Move in and shoot him. We got this here rifle and the Colt.'

'We'll have to scout around first. Find out where he is and how to do it. Then what? A bullet in the back, or what?'

'Sure thing. We'll git him before he gits his hand to his gun. Best way. He used to be pretty fast as I remember.'

The bullet in the back idea did not appeal to Sam although he saw the good sense in it. Facing up to Lewis, knowing what his draw was like, would be to court disaster. He had never thought of it this way in prison. It had always seemed simple enough. In his mind, he had always seen Lewis dropping to the ground with a slug in the head, quick and easy, and no questions asked. Now it was more complicated. There was the law for one thing. There must be a sheriff in Red Lance or somewhere not so far off who would want to know who had done it and why — and there was the prospect of a trial and a possible hanging thereafter.

The thought made Sam squirm. He had seen enough of the law to last a lifetime. If they were caught like before, the gallows would be a certainty. Lewis was not a criminal in the eyes of the world. There was no way of proving he had ever been outside the law and there was no legal excuse for the bullet in the back scenario.

It would have to be done in secrecy and there must be a quick getaway. It was all beginning to taste bad. Nerves seemed to jump and twang in his mind as he thought of it.

'When we git this over,' he observed, 'I aim to go straight, real straight, from then on. Sure, Lewis deserves what he's goin' to git but after that, I'll be avoiding the law and prison like the goddamned plague, I can tell you!'

'Yeah? How the hell you goin' to go straight? What do you think you'll live on? Air or what?'

'I'll git work. Maybe on a farm or with cattle.'

'You won't make much of a living piling hay or pushing cattle. Anyhow, nobody will give you work. Not with that haicut! Karl told you about all that.'

'Hair grows pretty quick. In a week

or two we'll look like we never saw prison.'

'Maybe. Well, I've got other plans. I didn't spend ten years of my life in the penitentiary just to spend the rest of it spreading manure, with some god-damned farmer yelling in my ear. No sirree! I got more ambition!'

They were silent for some minutes, each thinking of what the other had said, then Sam sat up sharply in the saddle.

'Jest thinking, when we git to Red Lance, I'll have to be careful. We need to think about what Karl said. Thing is, that feller who had this horse worked in the mine. Stands to reason, he must have been in the township often enough, and there's sure to be some folks around who can recognize it. It could be real troublesome.'

Thady whistled. 'You're right! Tell you something, for a guy talking about going straight, you're making one helluva start, riding around on a stolen horse and wearing a stolen gun!'

'The feller's dead!'

'Yeah, but he didn't mention you in his will.'

Sam fell silent once again. It was as if there was a blackness rising up on the trail in front of him and blocking out all his future. In his heart, he wanted things to work out the right way. He could still see Julia's eyes smiling at him as they had done that day on the buckboard.

'I'll go into the town first,' said Thady. 'I need to git some ammo for this rifle. That feller only had about six rounds. Could need a lot more than that. Another thing, we need hats.' He wiped the sweat from his sunburned forehead. 'Might be able to buy these things. There's bound to be a store in the place.'

'Put a bit of cloth around your head when you go in. It'll cover your haircut and there's a good excuse for it in this heat. If you like, though, we kin change horses and I'll go in first.'

'I'll do it,' insisted Thady.

When they saw a hint of smoke in the sky ahead, Sam stopped and watched Thady ride off around the corner of the trail. Then he drew his horse aside and moved into the nearest clump of trees. There he dismounted, ready for a long wait.

When Thady reached the township, he saw that it wasn't much of a place, amounting to little more than a double row of rough wooden buildings, one dingy saloon and a small store. There were a few people hanging about, all of whom stared at him curiously. There were two men sitting on the sidewalk near the store and a couple of others on the other side of the street against the window of the saloon. He was on the alert but all seemed peaceful enough.

As he tied his horse in front of the store he heard one of the men on the other side of the street speak in a sharp tone. He glanced over as they began to move towards him. At the same time, he was aware of a creaking as men got up from the wooden sidewalk just behind where he stood.

The muzzle of a gun pushed into his back.

'This here thumb-buster,' growled a voice, 'will only go off if you make it. Don't git excited. Here, Andy, take the rifle!'

In another moment they were joined by the men from the saloon. One of them, heavily built, with a dark moustache, slipped between Thady and the horse and thrust a gun into his ribs.

'You look like one of the guys we're waiting for,' he explained. 'Strangers are easy enough to pick out around here. Take that thing off his head, Andy.'

The rag was roughly torn away. There came a throaty chuckle.

'Hey, that's some haircut! Feller's been near enough scalped! How's that?'

'Jailbird! Them cons are crawling all over with lice. That's why. Keep back if ya don't want to mix the breed! Haw, haw!'

'Never mind that!' snapped the man with the moustache. 'Hey you!' The revolver dug deeper into Thady's ribs. 'Where's your partner? Mr Lewis said there was two of you.'

Thady's heart was in his boots. For a moment he could not answer, then he gritted his teeth.

'He ain't here — '

'Don't git smart!'

'I mean he ain't hereabouts at all. He went off way back. Long ways from here.'

'Yeah? Why was that?'

'We had an argument. He went his way.'

'That so? Where he go?'

'Who knows? He was real sore. He went off without speaking.'

'You three men ride around the place,' commanded the man with the moustache. 'See if there's another stranger about. Let's have that rifle, Andy . . . Hey! This has Joe's initial on the stock! Mr Lewis said about Joe being killed!' He spat suddenly, fiercely, into Thady's face. 'You dirty, murdering skunk! You'll git skewered for this!'

They took the road out of the town, Thady mounted on the roan but surrounded by the little throng of riders. Soon the path narrowed to a track which wound its way up a steep incline, hemmed in by fir trees. Then the workings of the mine came into view; a derrick with a wheel, water chutes, piles of cleared-out ore dirt. There were miners shovelling, lifting and carrying. Mules stood by, harnessed to small carts.

The track climbed still higher until they reached the house of the owner, perched on a height overlooking the little valley. It was not large but was well built of red sandstone. The front door was made of polished oak and there were curtains in the windows. Somehow it seemed out of place here, not many yards from the dirt and noise of the mine.

The door was opened by a middle-aged woman and the heavy, moustached man went in. He reappeared a moment later and motioned Thady to enter.

When Thady entered the room he gave an involuntary gasp of surprise. The walls were finely panelled and there was a stone fireplace with some expensive ornaments of brass. An oriental silk screen stood upon a thick carpet, while a picture of Abraham Lincoln hung above the fireplace. In the centre of the room was a shining deal table with an unlit brass oil-lamp upon it. Lewis sat at a desk by the window, half-silhouetted against the light.

For a moment Thady did not recognize Lewis. The grey-haired, hunched figure did not seem to resemble the tall, lithe man he remembered. In return, Lewis looked steadily at Thady, reflecting that he appeared much the same except for a roughness in his face which had not been there before. It had been a long time, but he could recollect quite a lot about this man, who, with his friend, had fallen for the trick with the bank. Thady, he believed, was not of the brightest; fairly easily led, and often naïve enough to think that a smile could only cover good humour. He was also greedy for money and had a streak of ruthlessness which came to the surface from time to time.

Such a man might be useful to Lewis, not in the mine, but perhaps in some of his other dealings which crossed the border of legality and called for brutality, even murder. One advantage Thady had was that he was quite expendable. If he was killed, no one would care, and few questions would be asked. He decided to give Thady a short trial, if he was willing to co-operate. If not, he would be disposed of at once.

'It's been a long time, Thady,' he said. 'Good to see you. Let go his arm, Jem, we're old friends. Sit down there. Make yourself comfortable.'

Pushed into a chair by Jem, Thady stared, at a loss for words, then he found his voice.

'Friends? That ain't exactly the way I remember it. Why, the last time I saw you — '

'Forget about the last time, Thady,'

interrupted Lewis. 'That was all just a mix-up. My gun went off when my horse jumped. Then things got out of hand. It was too bad what happened to you and your young friend but that's all over with. Now we kin start afresh.'

'Yeah?' answered Thady hesitantly. He was looking at Lewis from a different angle now, closer to, and saw the pain-worn face and the two sticks leaning against the desk.

'You're beginning to see it all, Thady. I kin get up from this chair and hobble around a bit but not much else. Got a bad injury a long time ago. Ain't the feller I used to be. You kin see that. Truth is, I've been expecting you. I remembered you would be out soon,' lied Lewis, 'and I hoped you'd drop in.'

There was silence. Thady did not know what to say. This meeting was different in every way from anything he had imagined.

'One thing, Thady,' drawled Lewis. 'Things look kind of bad for you right now. This rifle you're carrying has Joe

Maxwell's initial and there are men ready to swear it was his. If we bring in Sheriff Burns from Sweetholm you'll be hanging from a rope within a week. He don't waste much time with outlaws.' Lewis studied Thady's expression and then continued. 'But we don't have to do that. That young friend of yours, who I hear rode out on you, shot Joe, that right? He went off on Joe's horse and with Joe's handgun too.'

'Well . . . '

'No need to cover up for him, Thady, though it's loyal of you. He ain't worth it.'

'But how do you know . . . ?'

'I got people all around who tell me about interesting happenings. Anyway, it don't seem to be your fault. How would you like to work for me? I'll pay you better money than you've ever seen. I feel I should make things up to you after what you've been through. You could do real well and become a big man.'

Thady was nonplussed and did not

know how to reply. This was not the Lewis he had known before and had cursed every day in prison. What Lewis now said sounded like the best offer Thady had had in his life . . .

At about the same time as Thady was turning things over in his mind, Sam stood up amongst the trees by the trail, several miles from Starlight mine. He was becoming anxious and impatient as he waited for his partner to return.

He reckoned it must be some hours since Thady had ridden off in the direction of the town. There were dangers in that place, as they had both recognized. He himself could not sit around for ever in this clump of trees. It was necessary that he should do something to help his friend if things had gone wrong.

He mounted the bay and rode with caution towards Red Lance. When he reached the outskirts, he left the horse tied to a railing and went forward on foot. He was convinced now that the horse was a dead give-away in the vicinity of the mine. He could only hope it would still be there when he returned.

As he passed the first few buildings, he did his best to look casual, as if there was nothing at all on his mind. He was aware of the stares of people who stood at doorways or were busy attending to their daily chores. There seemed little doubt that he was as conspicuous as a duck amongst the chickens but he could only walk on until, within minutes, he came to the general store to which Thady had been heading.

Everything seemed quiet. There were one or two men loitering on the sidewalk down the street but that was all. Sam went into the store, which was small and full of everything imaginable from cheese to pickaxe handles. A short, balding man was behind the counter. He looked closely at Sam as he entered and his expression changed rapidly from surprise to suspicion. Sam felt there was no point in beating about the bush.

'Excuse me, but have you seen a feller around here with a checked shirt maybe about thirty-five years old?'

'Could be,' answered the storekeeper. His eyes had wandered to the gun at Sam's belt and his shoulders jumped nervously. 'He was outside. Went off with some fellers up to Starlight.'

'Went off?'

'Well, they took him. Seemed like they were waiting for him.'

'He just went with them?'

'Sounded like Mr Lewis wanted to see him. Nobody argues with Mr Lewis. I think they was expecting another guy too.' He bit his lip suddenly as if wishing he had said less. 'Anyhow, he ain't here.'

Sam left the store abruptly, stood irresolutely for a second, and then began to walk back the way he had come. He glanced behind once to see the storekeeper on the sidewalk pointing after him. He heard someone shouting something about Mr Lewis and the strangers. He went on rapidly until he reached the fence on the edge of the town where he had left the bay. To his immense relief, it was still there. As he mounted, a couple of men appeared from behind a building.

'Hey, that looks like Joe's horse, ain't it? I'd know that white fetlock any-wheres!' yelled one. 'How come that stranger's got it?'

'I heard somethin' about Joe being killed! Andy said something!' yelped the other. 'Hey, you! Git off that horse!' A hand went for a gun at his belt but Sam already had him covered by the Colt, and he dropped his arm.

Sam galloped out of the town as fast as the bay could move. He continued down the trail until the yells and shouts died away. Then he took the first chance to leave the worn track and turned up through the woods until he felt well hidden.

He remained still and tense and waited until he heard horsemen pass on the trail at some distance, their voices gradually receding.

Only when he was sure they had gone did he turn in the direction where he guessed the silver mine might be. He walked the horse with care through the trees, climbing the slopes by degrees, always moving towards the west.

It seemed a long time later when he heard the clanking of some kind of machine and scented smoke through the resinous pines. He tied the horse then and crept forward with great care. He saw the mine workings and the fine house on the hill. He also observed the guards strolling around with rifles at the ready. He studied the situation with a sinking heart, the conviction growing that he could do nothing to help Thady. If he attempted to attack he would be gunned down at once. Any appeal to the tender mercies of Lewis, he believed, could end only in his own death. He would not see Thady but might well lie beside him in the same grave.

He felt sure that Thady had already been killed. Lewis had somehow learned of their coming and decided to finish them off before they could cause trouble. He had missed Sam only by chance.

It was very likely that Thady was already dead. There could be no reason in the mind of Lewis for keeping him alive. The conviction sickened Sam to the heart. He turned away and crept back to his horse.

As he rode, his mind plunged into dark despair. What was he to do now? Was it possible for him to find his own way into a new life and leave Thady unavenged? He knew that was impossible for him but he felt powerless against Lewis and his henchmen. Mind in turmoil, he travelled throughout the day. Without thinking, he was going east, ever east. At length he knew why that was so. He had heard there were towns not so far to the east, larger than Red Lance, where he could find a sheriff and put the whole story to him. In that way there might be an investigation and some justice might come out of it. Lewis could be made to answer for the fate of Thady.

At the same time, he knew that he himself must answer for the death of Joe Maxwell, and that could go hard with him considering he still rode Joe's horse and Joe was buried like a dog beside the trail.

Karl and Julia might speak for him, if they could be found and if they were willing, but he had little hope that any good would come out of it. Lewis had the mine and Red Lance in his hands. Numerous witnesses could be brought forward to praise Joe as a fine, upstanding man and their voices must drown out any testimony of a guy, like himself, just out of jail.

As the sun went down, he found a place where there was sweet grass for his mount. He lay on the ground with the saddle under his head and spent much of the night in despairing dreams. He fell asleep sometime before dawn and awoke with the hot sun dragging him into harsh day.

7

The Osage came in sight of the wagon at about midday. He felt that the spirits were with him in that he had come across it within two days. It might have been much longer. His fellow tribesman, he knew, was still searching much further south, carrying the same message as he was, for Lewis had wanted to find the snake-oil man with all speed.

The Osage had ridden quickly on his piebald pony, sometimes asking for help from whites he passed on the trail. Some of them had been willing to speak to him and one such man had told him of the whereabouts of the wagon.

As he approached he was careful to give no sign of offence, knowing the suspicion with which an Indian was likely to be regarded, and held up a hand in peace to the old man and the girl on the buckboard. When he saw the grey head nod, he came nearer and handed over the small sheet of paper with the sign talk which Lewis had given him.

He waited patiently while the old snake-oil man read it. Lewis had told him to wait for an answer. He watched as the white man gasped in surprise, bit his lip and scowled in barely controlled anger. Then a pencil was produced and a hasty message scribbled on the back of the sheet.

The Osage accepted it and rode back the way he had come, not all the way to the Starlight mine but only about an hour's ride to the spot where Two-Tree stream ran into the river known to white people as the Wichita. There he met Hendrix and his band of men, as had been arranged.

Hendrix read the note quickly but carefully as Lewis had instructed. It stated simply: *I am not coming, Condor. See you some other time.*

Hendrix tightened his mouth under his heavy moustache. It was the reply

Lewis had more than half-expected. Karl had read the friendly invitation to enter into partnership or — if that was not acceptable — to meet his old antagonist gun to gun, but had seen in his imagination the words 'treachery' and 'double-cross' between the lines.

'OK, so it needs to be the other way,' said Hendrix to himself, and waved on his mounted men to follow him.

After the departure of the Indian, Karl was deep in thought, staring ahead over the heads of the team. Beside him, Julia looked at him anxiously. She had learned of the contents of the note and it scared her. At the same time, she felt the deep anger and hatred which had been in her soul since the terrible day of her mother's ordeal and death. When Joe Maxwell had appeared on the trail, all the suffering of that day had come back to her. As she had stared at his bloody corpse, she had known satisfaction and horror mixed with the hope that all was now over.

Now she knew there was more to

come. Karl had become aware of the whereabouts of this man — Condor or Lewis — and would seek revenge. She had no clear memory of Lewis but realized now that he had been one of that loathsome gang on that fearful day. As such, she condemned him to death in her heart, but was afraid of the consequences for Karl, who would seek his enemy out at a time and place of his own choosing. The idea filled her with dread as Karl might not survive. If he did not, she vowed to kill Lewis herself or die in the attempt.

Karl did not speak for a long time as the team plodded on unhurriedly. He mulled over the fact that Lewis and his old enemy, Condor, were one and the same. He had seen the name of Lewis on the pay-check he had found on Maxwell but had thought nothing of it. Now he knew where Condor was and he felt determined to settle with him as long as the young girl could be made safe before then. He must find a secure place where she could stay while he dealt with Condor. Also, there was the added complication of these two young fellers making for the mine in the expectation of finding work . . .

Or was that what they were really after? He had always doubted their yarn about looking for work as miners. Who could tell what kind of confusion they might create with Condor — or Lewis — or whatever else he was calling himself?

Anyway, there was nothing he could do about them now. He needed to look out for himself and Julia. He reckoned it would take some hours for the Indian to get back to Lewis with the return message. After that, Lewis might decide to send out some of his henchmen to settle things. It would be wise not to be caught out on the open trail but there was a township not so far ahead which he could reach long before the Indian reached Starlight.

He snapped the reins and the team increased its pace just a little . . .

In the late afternoon, with the help of the Osage scout, Hendrix was near to catching up with the wagon. He kept his little troop of men well back and out of sight until the Osage signalled that the wagon was turning a bend in the trail so that Karl could not see far behind. At that, Hendrix left most of his men and rode at a trot with only two of his followers a short distance in the rear.

He caught up swiftly with the wagon and waved cheerfully to Karl at the reins.

'Hey, mister, can you tell me how to git to Sweetholm? Seems I've lost my way somehow.'

'Sweetholm?' repeated Karl. He was taken by surprise by the sudden appearance of the horseman alongside. 'You missed the turning, way back . . . '

★ ★ ★

He had no time to finish giving directions. Hendrix lunged with the swiftness of a lynx and grabbed at the older man's sleeve. At the same time, he spurred his horse forward and in a second Karl had been pulled from the buckboard and had fallen violently almost under the wheels.

He attempted to struggle to his feet but another rider was there and a club swung hard on to the back of his skull. He went down as if poleaxed to the earth.

On the other side of the wagon, Julia made to snatch up the rifle but Andy was on hand to strike out with his pistol. The blow went home with paralysing force on her arm and she rolled in pain on the buckboard while Andy, with a grin, grabbed the rifle as a trophy for himself.

Within minutes, Karl had been thrown over the back of a riderless horse. Andy and the Osage hung back for a moment as if to seek plunder but were waved on by Hendrix who knew that Lewis did not want time wasted.

'Let's go!' he yelled. 'We're due back at Starlight!'

For a moment it was as if the Osage meant to disobey the command, as he snatched Karl's black hat from the ground to put on his own head, but then the cavalcade went off in a thunder of hoofs.

After they had gone came silence but for the idling movements of the team and the soft moaning of Julia as she nursed her arm and began to face the enormity of what had happened.

How long it was before the pain eased and she took stock of her situation, she had no way of telling. Gradually, it came to her that for the first time she was without the protection of the man who had taken her in as a wounded and distraught child. For long minutes she was overcome with despair but slowly the worst of her distress was replaced by a cold determination to do anything she could to help Karl, regardless of the cost to herself.

She knew these men were heading for the mine and were in the pay of Lewis. She knew also that the mine was not far from Red Lance and it seemed to her there was no alternative but to go there now and to find a way to save Karl or to kill Lewis. In her heart she saw only failure, but the greater failure would be to do nothing. That, in itself, could lead only to a living death.

She turned the wagon and drove on through the dusk and the night until the horses stopped from fatigue. She allowed them rest and made sure they were fed but could find no rest herself. At first light, she was again on her way, weary but filled with fiery determination.

It was with some surprise that she came in sight of Jason's homestead. She had almost forgotten its existence. In the past she had been there with Karl; once for a horse and another time for water when a barrel in the wagon had sprung a leak. She remembered the unsavoury Jason and how he had looked at her. She would have gone on but for the need she had now, which was for a gun . . . a gun with which to kill Lewis even if she failed to help Karl.

Jason came out to meet her as she drove in through the gate. He looked very surprised to see her at the reins instead of Karl. At first he seemed to believe that Karl must be inside, out of sight under the canvas for some reason, and his eye kept moving in that direction as he spoke to her.

'Well, what a pleasure it is to see you, missy! Jest as pretty as ever, that's for sure! How kin I help?'

'I want to buy a gun,' she replied. There seemed no way of asking in a more subtle manner. 'A rifle and a handgun too, if you have it. I've got enough money.'

'Sure, sure, I know you and Karl always deal fair and square. How come you're needing guns? Running into trouble with Injuns or something?' He laughed flatly at his own joke 'I thought you and Karl always went armed. Got to these days out on the trail, no doubt about it.'

'We need guns. I lost the rifle. Do you have guns you can sell or don't you?' she rapped impatiently.

'Hey, Karl, what kind of rifle do you want?' Jason called out loudly, suspicion in his voice. 'I got a pretty good Winchester.'

'Karl isn't here,' Julia had to admit. 'He won't be long. He's following on another horse,' she added as a hopeful lie.

'Not like him,' answered Jason. 'Something wrong, missy? If I kin help, I will. Jest tell me.'

Julia stared at him, tears not far from her eyes. God, how she could do with an ally! She had always disliked and distrusted Jason. She hated him, hated his leering looks and his smell. Maybe, though, she had been unfair. He had never really done her any harm. She studied him, trying to see into his mind, but saw nothing but darkness . . .

'Please, just sell me a gun,' she pleaded. 'That's all I want. I'll pay well. That Winchester sounds about right.'

Jason was silent. Then he walked round the back of the wagon and returned. He was looking at the ground, seemingly busy with his thoughts. When he glanced up at her there came a strange light into his eye.

'OK,' he said quietly. 'Come over to the cabin and I'll show you the rifle. I got handguns too.'

'Bring them out here,' she replied. 'I've no time to waste.'

Jason looked at the sky and then glanced at an Indian youth by the fence.

'Hey, Choctaw, get around to the back paddock and attend to the white like I told you!' He turned to grin at Julia. 'Goddamned Injun, keeps forget-tin' everything! Listen here, missy, we kin talk better inside. You could do with coffee or something. You look bushed.'

'Hand me out the gun and ammunition. That's all I ask.' Julia struggled to keep control of her trembling voice. 'I won't argue about the price.'

'Jest git down off that wagon.' Jason's tone changed to a threat. 'Come inside with me.'

He made to snatch at her dress. She lashed out with the slack of the reins across the back of his hand.

'Don't git smart!' he snarled and reached up to grab her about the waist. She struck him again but his arms gripped her tightly and began to drag her from the buckboard. Beyond his bulky form, she saw the young Indian running forward. He made an attempt to pull Jason away but with a curse Jason swung round and punched him hard on the mouth. The youth fell and Julia attempted to urge the team into motion but Jason still held her and in a moment they were both on the ground, Julia in sudden agony as her bad arm took the force of the fall.

Then he renewed his grip around

her waist and half-carried, half-dragged her towards the cabin. They reached the door and he stopped to turn the handle. For a second his grip was less secure and she jerked away from him and tumbled through the swinging door to the interior.

Instinctively, she pushed her back against it, holding him outside while she gasped for breath. But then his shoulder thundered on the wood and he was inside with her . . .

Outside, the young Choctaw had pulled himself to his feet. For a moment he stood indecisively, staring in horror at the cabin. He was afraid of Jason for good reason, having felt his fist often enough before. Also, Jason was armed and would not hesitate to kill a mere Indian boy who angered him in a matter such as this.

The lad looked around at a complete loss as to what to do. He heard the girl's voice raised in panic. At the same time, he saw a movement on the hillside to the west. He ran then, like the wind, and leaped upon his pony.

Sam, riding wearily into what he knew was an uncertain future, had seen Jason's place and had decided to skirt round it. When he saw the Indian galloping towards him he sat up and and reached for his gun. Then he heard the youth shouting: 'Come! Come!' and saw him turn the pony to ride back to the homestead. At the same moment, Sam saw the wagon. He forced his mount into a gallop and overtook the Indian, entering the gate some distance in advance.

He could hear Julia screaming and needed no telling about what was happening. The door burst open under his right boot. Julia was on the floor with Jason panting and cursing on top of her. Her dress had been ripped. Jason's clothes were in disarray, his fat sweaty back uppermost, his face for the moment concealed.

He twisted round, just the same, at Sam's abrupt entrance. A hand stretched towards the gunbelt lying on the floor. Sam drew his side-gun but hesitated, suddenly realizing that the bullet might go right through Jason's body and hit Julia. His brain was, nevertheless, on fire with savage fury. He swung the weapon at Jason's bald head but before it struck, the man suddenly jerked and screamed, twisted as if to pull himself away and then lay still.

Sam stood as if suddenly frozen. There came no sound but Julia's sobbing as she turned face down to the floor. The Indian youth stood in the doorway, eyes wide.

Then Sam reached out a hand to Julia but did not touch her, knowing she could tolerate the hands of no man at that moment. Instead, he said foolishly:

'It's all right. You're all right.'

Slowly she ceased shivering and pulled her torn dress across her body. Her face was distorted and ugly with fear and loathing. Her arms were badly bruised and there was a bleeding scratch on her neck. Sam did not attempt to speak again but gripped Jason by the heels and pulled him through the door and around the corner of the cabin. As he did so, the body turned and Sam saw the knife embedded just under the ribs.

He stared for a moment and then withdrew it. Blood dripped from the blade. For some minutes he could not move, then he went round to the front of the shack again and stopped motionless as he saw Julia. Regardless of her surroundings, she had taken off her dress and stood in her under-clothes. He saw her dip the blood-soaked garment into the water butt and wring it out, doing her best to clean it, before the blood could dry. She seemed oblivious to his presence. Her face was tense and her eyes full of disgust.

He turned and retreated once again round the corner of the building, where he waited some minutes before ventur-ing to approach her. She was now standing tensely in the sunlight, wearing her soaked dress, now seemingly cleansed of blood. He held out the knife to her but she shook her head and stared into the sky. He dropped her knife into the water butt.

'Thank you,' she said, glancing in his direction. For a moment he thought she was thanking him for attempting to save her but then realized she was glad he had removed the corpse. He felt like congratulating her on dealing with Jason herself but knew she did not want that. It was as if she had been in the grip of a boa constrictor and there was nothing to do but try to thrust the hellish experience out of mind.

She told him all that had happened on the day before: the Osage, the message, the ambush by Hendrix, and of her resolve to get to Red Lance to do what she could. She spoke calmly and quietly and with a hard determination. Sam listened carefully, understanding fully her feelings, but with no hope that she could achieve anything. He knew better, though, than to attempt to dissuade her, and he recognized within himself the need to follow the same course.

'I want to come with you,' he said simply. 'I have things to settle too.' He told her about Thady and what had happened in the past with Lewis. As he spoke, he realized fully that he had given up all idea of bringing in the law. There was another dead man to explain and time was running out. Julia needed his help at once. He would go with her, no matter what the consequences.

They found the Winchester Jason had been talking about. It was new, with excellent repeater action and there was a box of ammunition. There was another rifle too, a Henry repeater, old but serviceable. There were two or three handguns also, heavy, bone-shattering killers. Julia took a Colt .45 and hung it from a belt at her waist.

'That gun's got some recoil,' warned Sam. 'It takes a strong wrist to use it.'

'The Peacemaker, as they call it,'

answered Julia. 'Karl made his own kind of peace with it. Maybe I'll bring more peace to the world when I finish Lewis with this.'

When they left the cabin they saw that the Indian had unhitched the horses from the wagon and let them loose in the paddock. In their place, he had saddled Jason's white, a fine, strong animal, and had brought out a grey which Jason had kept out of sight. He had released Joe Maxwell's bay, which was now weary, into the paddock with the animals from the wagon.

'I come with you,' he said gravely. 'I hear what you say about Lewis and I know about dogs like Jason. I have a rifle too and can lead you quick way. You trust me?'

They looked into his brown eyes and could not help trusting him. He nodded when he saw their expressions and dismounted to help Julia into the saddle. She sat astride, regardless of her dress, her spirit uplifted at his offer of friendship and help.

'What's your name?' asked Sam.

'Porcupine,' came the answer, after a moment of struggling with translation. 'Him . . . ' He jerked his head back to where Jason's feet protruded round the corner of the shack. 'He call me only tribal name. Big fool man.'

With few words they set off for Starlight, the young Choctaw in the lead. After some miles the trail became steep and narrow, hemmed in by trees. The going was rough and progress became slower. Julia slumped in the saddle. Sam knew she had not slept in two days. He brought her horse to a halt and insisted she dismount. In a short while she lay still, breathing lightly, her face calm for the first time.

When they continued on their way the sun was already in its swift descent, casting long shadows from rocks overhanging the track, which now led through a gully. After a time, Sam glanced back to see the figure of an Indian riding quietly a short distance in the rear. He halted, gun already in hand. At that moment, Porcupine turned also and rode back to face the newcomer.

There was a short conversation, incomprehensible to Sam, and then the young Choctaw turned to explain.

'He Iron Eyes. Him Osage. Work for Lewis. He has some days searched for the snake-oil man. I tell him now Lewis makes wise old man prisoner. This Iron Eyes has seen young white woman before in towns. He frien — '

'What's he doing now?' asked Sam suspiciously.

'Go back to Lewis.'

'Not likely!' snapped Sam, suddenly alarmed. His gun was pointing at the chest of the Osage. 'He must stay with us. We don't want that coyote knowing we're on our way!'

The Osage said something to Porcupine, who turned to translate.

'He say he think snake-oil man good. Makes good medicine. But Iron Eyes work for Lewis and goes back.'

'I can't have that,' growled Sam.

132

'He'll give us away.'

The Osage seemed to understand and glared into Sam's face, his eyes suddenly explaining his name.

'Shoot! Only small man kill friend. Iron Eyes never afraid. No one tell Iron Eyes to stay or not to stay!'

He turned his horse aside and left the trail, riding up a slope into the trees. Sam could not raise his gun to shoot him in the back.

'Well,' he said, 'that's like sending up a smoke signal and I didn't have the guts to stop him!'

'Guts isn't the same as cold-blooded killing,' answered Julia, 'but you're right; this gives us even less of a chance.'

But she did not think of giving up and urged her mount into greater speed.

8

Lewis leaned against the fence in the morning sun, a short distance from his house, at a point overlooking his mine workings. All was quiet. There was no hammering or whirl of machinery and no human voices. On the previous evening he had announced a paid holiday for his workers in honour of his mother's birthday. They had been surprised for he was not known for his generosity, and it had never occurred to anyone that he had a mother. Nevertheless, they had accepted the break from work without question and with evident delight. Even his housekeeper had been sent to visit her sister in Red Lance. Lewis wanted privacy today and had retained only those men he could really trust.

He had something special to do. He was going to kill his old enemy, Karl.

He had not yet quite made up his mind how he was going to do it. There had been no sleep for him all night, partly because of his pain but mostly on account of a mind that seethed with excitement and anticipation. Also, there was anger and a sense of frustration. He had spoken with Karl in the afternoon just after the latter had been brought in as a prisoner. It had not been a satisfactory interview. Karl had shown anger and defiance but there was no fear. The grey eyes had stared at Lewis as if he had crawled from under a stone.

That had to change. The snake-oil man must squirm before he died, otherwise, it seemed to Lewis, the victory was not complete.

He had thought of shooting and hanging but did not really believe that these methods could change the expression in Karl's eyes. Any such death might well be too quick for such a man.

There was burning. He had thought of slow burning. The idea had come into his mind as he saw the Osage horseman riding down to the mine workings still wearing Karl's black hat. It was an old Indian way. It could be made to last for days, only Lewis did not have the time. Some hours would have to do.

He made his decision.

'Hey, Andy,' he called. 'Git that iron frame these miners use for grilling beef. Bring it up here and set a good fire under it.'

Lewis watched as Andy fixed up the rough iron barbecue and began to gather kindling and logs under it, whistling in his youthful way as he did so. It was apparent that Andy had not quite got the idea. Probably he guessed that the boss was going to eat grilled steak in the absence of the meals usually prepared by his housekeeper. Lewis smiled with grim humour. Well, he would find out soon enough. Right now there was another thing to see to . . . that Thady feller. How much could he be trusted?

He shuffled around to the other side of the house where there was a wide space, covered in grass which was kept short by one of the labourers. It was mostly surrounded by clumps of pine trees at about a hundred yards' distance. A short distance away was a shed and a small, broken-down cart but there was little else in the field.

Outside the shed sat one of his guards, drinking coffee from an enamel mug. Two more men were keeping a general look-out over beside the trees. Lewis always had it in the back of his mind that there might be somebody gunning for him. It was an old habit that died hard. Today he was more uneasy than usual.

'Hey, Mac,' he said to the man by the shed, 'keep on your feet. You got a prisoner in there. Anyhow, I want him out now. Let's see how smart he's looking this morning!'

Mac rose reluctantly, emptying the dregs of his coffee on the ground. It did not seem to him that the prisoner needed careful guarding, being an old guy who had already been roughed up, but he hid his thoughts from the boss.

When Karl was brought out into the sunlight, he blinked after the darkness of the shed where he had spent the night on the earthen floor. His jacket was crumpled and torn. His grey hair was dishevelled. His lip was cut from a punch he had taken from Hendrix and his head still throbbed from the club blow which had rendered him unconscious.

'Not just at your best today, hey, Karl?' Lewis smirked. 'You ain't looking too good!'

'You don't look like much yourself,' retorted Karl, forcing a grin.

'It was your bullet that reduced me to what I am now,' said Lewis bitterly. 'Keep that in mind.'

'Too bad it didn't blow you away altogether. It would have saved everybody a heap of trouble.'

Lewis stared, his eyes cold. He had decided not to mention the fire until later. Any man would rather take a bullet than face that and he didn't want Karl attempting anything that would set guns blazing. The prisoner needed to be trussed up like a hog. Only then would the defiant light go out of his eyes.

'Your troubles are only just starting, snake-oil man!' rasped Lewis.

Karl shrugged. He had no expectations of surviving this day.

'Talking about snakes, you were always a low rattler, Condor. Money ain't made you no better.'

'Tell Thady to come here!' shouted Lewis to a man near the house. 'I got a job for him!'

Thady came out, looking worried. Karl stared at him in astonishment, having had no notion of his presence. Thady already knew that Karl had been brought in. He had witnessed it from the window of the tiny bedroom which Lewis had allowed him to use until his worth as a loyal employee could be assessed. He had been under guard, too, although he was unaware of it.

Now he looked at the ground because it was not easy to face Karl Plinston.

'OK,' said Lewis. 'Take this polecat over to the cart. I want his feet tied to the wheel just in case he has any idea of making a break for it. Here's a handgun for you, Thady — Navy pistol, pretty good. It shoots straight.'

Karl was hustled over to the cart to which Mac tied his feet. Lewis watched as Thady followed with some suggestion of reluctance. The Navy pistol hung loosely in his hand. Lewis knew it contained only one bullet. The first pull of the trigger would fire it: after that there would be only the clicking of an empty chamber. By then, however, he would know about Thady.

The two men over by the trees were walking slowly towards the little group, curiosity overcoming, for the moment, their fear of Lewis's disapproval, but ready to stop where they were should he yell out an order. The Osage in the black hat stood some short distance away looking on with calm detachment. Andy appeared round the corner of the house.

'Hey, Mr Lewis, the fire's starting up swell.'

'OK, Andy,' interrupted Lewis, 'let it blaze up real good. Now listen, Thady, you and me had a fine talk about you working for me. I promised to pay you real well and that I'd make up to you for that misunderstanding all them years ago. You can be richer than you've ever been in your whole life and then some!

'Thing is, though,' he went on, 'I need to know I can depend on you. This guy here is the same man as you travelled with a few days ago. Remember the snake-oil man? You admitted you had been thinking of helping yourself to some of the dough he swindles out of poor folks. Well, he's done a lot worse than that in his life. I reckon it's time he left this world so that he can meet his Maker and get judged. So I want you to shoot him.'

'What . . . ?'

'Shoot him but don't kill him right off. I want him to really feel what it's like taking a bullet. Give him the first one low down in the leg — the kneecap's a good place — sore as hell — then the rest where you like. But I want him dead.'

'Mr Lewis . . . '

'Look at him, Thady. You can't shoot a man unless you're looking at him. Go on. Fix your eyes on him.'

Thady looked. He met the gaze of Karl, cold with contempt, but without fear. Then Karl's hands, still free, went to the inside pocket of his torn jacket. Hendrix made a move forward, thinking there might be a hidden gun, but the hand came back out in a trice holding something that caught the light of the sun. It was a silver star, old and worn, which Karl quickly thrust into his lapel. He did not fix it properly. It hung loosely but shone in the sunlight.

'This is a badge, Condor, that I should never have let go of. I was a lawman once but messed it all up and I regret that more anything in my life. The law is what we need more than anything else, especially right now in a place like this where the wolves have taken over. Make this sap pull the trigger. He'll just be shooting at something better than himself, for the law is better than any of us.'

Thady stared. He had no liking for the law. It had always seemed to be against him and everything he did — but he had a respect for it.

'Cut the play-acting, Swigg-Hardy,' sneered Lewis. 'It don't cut no ice. Get on with it, Thady.'

'It don't seem right, Mr Lewis. He's unarmed and tied up. He's old too.'

The Navy pistol was still pointing at the ground. Lewis could see that Thady was not going to use it. He already had his hand on the butt of his own gun. It came up in a quick movement. There was a slight noise as the barrel left the leather holster and Thady began to turn his head to look. Lewis meant to kill

Thady with a bullet to the brain but his aim was not as good as it might have been in his youth. The bullet entered into the side of Thady's face, smashing out his teeth, and re-emerged through his right cheekbone. His head suddenly became a mass of blood and he went down to the crumpled grass, body twitching.

There came a sudden silence. The men standing nearby seemed stunned. Hardened though they were, this murder shocked them for a moment. No one moved or attempted to speak.

A short distance away the sunlight which had caught the silver star barely penetrated the woodland. Sam crouched there with Julia at his side. Somewhere over to his right was Porcupine, hidden in the shadows. Led by the young Choctaw, they had made their way through the dark to the vicinity of the mine, which they had reached just before dawn. The sun had risen as they had crouched in the trees, staring at the fine house over the stretch of grass, while they tried to figure out where Karl was being held and what they might do about it.

They had seen Lewis come out, helped by Hendrix and watched as he went around the other side of the building only to return a few minutes later. They had seen Karl being dragged from the shed and tied to the cart and Sam had gasped with astonishment at the sudden appearance of Thady.

Out of earshot as they were, they had heard nothing of the conversation. The death of Thady had left Sam stunned. He could not move but gripped his rifle in tight frustration, afraid to fire for fear of bringing about Karl's immediate execution.

'They're going to kill Karl!' Julia whispered hoarsely. She made as if to rise to her feet and stopped as Sam's hand came out to prevent her. Then he felt her grip his arm. 'When next you see me,' she said in the same low tones, fear setting her voice trembling. 'Do what you can. Anything to help Karl.'

She was off then, stumbling under the low branches, moving a little way further into the shelter of the woods as if desperate not to be seen. He opened his mouth to shout after her but did not give way to the impulse.

Out there on the sunlit grass Lewis still stood while his men stared. Hendrix was looking at the body on the ground. The two guards who had been near the trees were now motionless. Andy shifted from one foot to the other. Three other men had come from behind the house, rifles in hand, having heard the shot. The Indian in the black hat had not moved.

Anger was replacing the effects of shock in Sam's mind. To see Thady killed was about as much as he could stand. He drew a bead on Lewis but did not pull the trigger. He believed that to shoot now was to bring instant death to Karl. Then he saw the figure of an Indian emerge from the trees nearer to the house and begin to walk openly and slowly towards the cart to which Karl was bound. For a second, he thought it was Porcupine but then he recognized the Osage they had met on the trail through the woods,

Now, surely, they must be betrayed! All was lost! He raised his rifle again but halted the movement as he saw Karl stiffen and stare across the clearing. At the same time the other men present turned to look in the same direction. Lewis's head jerked in surprise. Andy jumped visibly. Sam twisted his head to look also but had to push a resinous twig of pine from his face before he saw her.

Julia had come out from the tree cover towards the other side of the clearing. She stepped forward a few yards and then stood still in full view of all.

The sunlight caught her youthful figure. Her black hair hung untidily on her shoulders and her dress was torn but, as always, she was beautiful. She did not move. No expression was on her pretty features, but Sam knew that her heart hammered within her breast.

Hendrix was the first man to move. Then came the others, beginning to pace towards her slowly, as if dumbfounded by the sudden apparition. Only Hendrix spoke once, loudly enough for Sam to hear.

'Hey, ain't that the gal from the wagon?'

They continued to advance towards her as if entranced, seeing her as young, beautiful and vulnerable. The thought coming into their minds was that she must not get away. Julia understood that as well as did Sam. She had known it before she made the fateful decision to show herself.

Her small fists were tightly gripped in a nervous spasm. It was as if she were back on that terrible day of long ago when she had seen her mother attacked and killed by men such as these, one of whom she knew was in the group which now menaced her. Her soul shivered uncontrollably. Her hatred of the men who now stared at her was matched only by her fear of them. She stood her ground, unmoving, as they approached.

Sam knew now what she had meant when she whispered: '*When next you see me, do what you can*. He glared back at Lewis, who was the only man who had not wandered from the place where Karl stood bound. His rifle came up but then he saw the Osage, Iron Eyes, bound forward, knife in hand, and bend to slash the rope that held Karl to the wheel.

The Osage with the black hat swung round but then stood still in surprise as he saw his fellow tribesman half-drag and half-carry the prisoner back towards the trees. A moment later he was walking quickly after Iron Eyes as if to ask what was happening. He did not get far. Lewis, seeing both Indians seemingly involved in the same act of treachery, fired quickly and the bullet found its target. The nearest Osage fell, the black hat tumbling from his head to the grass.

In that second Sam fired at Lewis.

His ill-considered aim missed by a yard but Lewis threw himself heavily to the ground. At the shot, all those men caught out in the open, almost instinctively made for cover. Most dropped to the grass. One man near the house dodged round the corner of the building but another, attempting to do the same, suddenly staggered and fell as a bullet came from the rifle of the young Choctaw, hidden under the pines.

The element of surprise and the uncertainty as to where the shots were coming from gave Iron Eyes the opportunity of pulling Karl under cover. Both fell to the ground and the Osage reached for the rifle he had already hidden at that spot. In his own mind he was not certain why he had taken this appalling risk to save the old white man. He had seen the snake-oil man before in the townships and respected him for his skill with medicines. Also, he had seen the girl and had been amused at her act of being an Indian princess — an idea quite foreign and foolish to his people.

Nevertheless, he had no great liking for whites and felt he owed them nothing. He worked for Lewis, as his cousin Red Feather did, simply to earn a little money to buy ammunition for his hunting rifle and a few items of clothing supplied by the traders. His reason for helping Karl was, he realized, simply pity, for he knew the black heart of Lewis and had seen the fire being lit.

Also, he had seen Sam and the Choctaw in the woods and had been expecting them to open fire. When he saw the girl emerge and all heads turn in her direction, it had seemed an opportunity. On an impulse, he had decided to try to save the snake-oil man but now his heart sank in despair as he realized that his action had cost Red Feather his life.

His rifle was already up to take revenge, but Lewis had dragged himself through the grass to his own house and was now sheltered by the porch.

Meanwhile, Sam had half-risen to his knees. His brain was on fire with anxiety over Julia. She had vanished into the shelter of the pines as swiftly as a deer but he was not sure where she now was. Two men who had approached most closely to her suddenly leaped up from the grass and ran to the trees. Sam cursed his own momentary lack of vigilance. These men, he knew, could not be far behind her.

In a second he was up and stumbling through the low-hanging branches in the direction she had last been seen. A shot rang out and his heart sank but then rejoiced as he made out the blue of her dress weaving towards him through the pines. He scrambled further forward and then dropped to one knee as he saw the figure of a man some distance behind her. He took quick aim and fired. The man vanished and then she was with him, panting and sobbing. He put his arms around her and held her close.

But there was no time for words of comfort. A man with blood pouring from a wound in his shoulder was but a short distance behind her, his face twisted in anger and pain. He seemed to have dropped his rifle but in his hand he held a knife. He grabbed Julia's arm while she writhed and screamed. The knife rose to strike. Julia's body blocked any chance of a shot from Sam but he leaped forward and gripped the man's wrist with both hands, forcing the knife back. In a second, they were wrestling furiously, branches whipping at their faces. The man was strong and Sam felt himself being overpowered. Then his foot caught a root and he fell back with his opponent almost on top of him.

Blood from the man's wound spattered Sam's face and entered his eyes but he saw the knife raised again, this time to deal a death blow.

Julia had staggered to one side but her hand felt the butt of her handgun in the holster behind her back, where she had concealed it before stepping out of the trees to face the men she so hated. Clumsily, she withdrew the Colt .45. Holding it in both hands she pulled the trigger. She took no time to aim. The heavy gun leaped from her hands with a violence that hurt her fingers but the shot went home, low in the body, and the man fell with an animal-like moan to the ground.

Julia stared. For a moment a wild jubilation and sense of triumph ran through her heart. She had saved Sam but she knew there was much more to her feelings than that. In killing this man it seemed to her she had also killed all of the past. The feeling of total despair which had so often crushed her spirit seemed to have been finally lifted. In its place came joy.

Then she heard him whimper as death overtook him and the joy went out of her. She stood once more in misery, her eyes wide but seeing nothing because of the dark shadow which seemed to envelop her mind.

'Thank God!' came Sam's voice. 'He

had me for dead meat. You saved my life.'

Julia nodded. Sam rose to his feet and took her arm. Looking into her face, he thought he understood.

'There was no other way,' he said.

In a moment she seemed to recover herself. She smiled briefly.

'You're still alive.'

'We both are. Come! We have to get to the horses.'

'No, we must get to Karl! That's why we came. He must be round this side of the wood.'

She ran, half-bent, under the branches. He followed quickly, shaking his head. His mind had been full of the need to save Julia. For some minutes he had forgotten Karl.

Almost unexpectedly they came across Karl and the two Indians, crouching behind a fallen log. Karl was grey with exhaustion. His face was tense but lightened a little when he saw Julia.

'My God, girl,' he breathed. 'I

thought you were dead. But you should have stayed away from here. Did I not try to make you have some sense? Now you've landed in the same bear-trap as the rest of us.'

'Bad time start soon,' confirmed Porcupine. 'All them crazy wolves move in to kill.'

9

All was silent but for an insect humming in the branches overhead. From where they crouched in the pinewoods, they could see only part of a rough stretch of grass and a corner of the building. For a moment there was no sign of their enemies.

'I reckon Lewis has slipped into the house,' growled Karl. 'Don't see any of the others. Polecat murdered your friend,' he added, glancing sideways at Sam.

'I saw it,' hissed Sam. His heart seemed to take an anguished dive. In that moment he remembered the long years he had spent with Thady in prison, their comradeship, and the support they had given to one another throughout the ordeal. He bit his lip, almost crying out in despair.

'I'll kill Lewis for that, believe me!

Right now, though, we need to git to the horses. We have to git Julia out of here as quick as hell!'

Karl looked at him closely and nodded. 'You're right. First things first. Revenge can wait.'

'Men between us and horses,' put in Porcupine in a grave whisper. 'I hear men over there under trees.'

Sam twisted his head to listen. He heard nothing but he did not doubt the young Choctaw's word.

'Well, we have to git past them. Come on! Let's go!'

'How many of these rats are we up against?' asked Karl, rising stiffly to his feet.'

'Maybe seven,' returned Sam in the same low voice. 'That includes the viper in the house. Julia downed one herself!'

He said the last part with a hint of pride but saw by her expression that she had mixed feelings about it. Killing was not in her nature, however justified it may have been.

'I need a gun,' said Karl. He was

handed the Colt that had belonged to Maxwell. The older man brightened a little as he held it in his hands. Then he straightened the silver badge in his lapel and made it secure. His eyes changed as he did so. There came a sudden gleam of pride through the anger.

At that instant a bullet smashed its way through the branches immediately above their heads, ripping bark and scattering pine needles. It had come from the direction of the house. Iron Eyes, still crouching behind the log, raised his rifle and then lowered it again, unable to get a clear view of the window.

Sam reached over and touched his shoulder with the intention of signalling that the Osage should come with them quickly but the Indian did not turn his head.

'Iron Eyes very angry,' whispered Porcupine. 'Lewis kill his cousin. He stay to fight.'

It was evident from the still intensity of the Osage that Porcupine was right.

Iron Eyes would stay and fight to the death. Sam pursed his mouth. It seemed to make their withdrawal very much harder but there was no help for it. What mattered was getting through to the horses and making an escape for Julia's sake, if that were at all possible. There was a good chance they would all lie dead pretty soon not far from Iron Eyes because the odds were stacked so much against them.

They moved with caution back to the spot where they thought they had left the horses. The Choctaw was in front, eyes and ears alert. They had not gone more than fifty yards when a shot rang from just ahead and the Indian threw himself to the ground. There came the sound of someone crashing through the undergrowth off to the left. Instinctively, Sam and Julia moved a little to the right. Just then, Julia's dress must have caught the light for another bullet sang past her head.

This one came from the old shed out on the grass where Karl had been held as a prisoner. Sam saw part of the body of a man thrust out from the corner and fired rapidly, scarcely taking time to aim. More by luck than good judgement, the rifle bullet went home and a man staggered into clear view clutching his shoulder. Then the Choctaw fired and the man went down with a bullet in the chest, screaming in pain and fear.

Sam drew Julia further into the shadows.

Outside in the sunlight, the dying man writhed in the grass. A short distance from him came a groan as if in answer to his screams. Thady hung somewhere in the twilight zone between death and life, his mind fighting for consciousness in the dark mist which enveloped it . . .

At that moment, Iron Eyes slipped from behind his shielding log and crept slowly towards the outskirts of the wood. The anger within him burned as if a flaming torch had been thrust into his body. He had seen his cousin, Red Feather, shot in the back by Lewis and the need to take revenge consumed him. As men, he and his cousin had never been alike. In spite of his name, Iron Eyes was not of an unkindly nature, whereas Red Feather, older by some years, had been hardened by his life experience. Such considerations made no difference. A fellow tribesman, who was a blood relative, had been shot down like a wild animal and Iron Eyes felt that bullet as if it had been fired at his own back.

Some yards across the grass was the end of the fine house which Lewis, in his new found prosperity, had proudly built for himself. There was a small window on that side and Iron Eyes knew Lewis was there, keeping out of sight, but with his rifle leaning on the edge of the sill, ready for action should any of his enemies show themselves.

Iron Eyes knew there was little chance of a successful shot by aiming at the small window, and a direct approach across the open space would be fatal. He therefore kept to the shelter of the trees and worked his way like a coyote along the edge of the wood until he reached a spot from which he could see along the back of the house.

There he saw the little garden which one of Lewis's Negroes cultivated for him and the narrow end of the shutters which stood open to allow air into the best room on this day of heat. He could also see the fence that skirted the top of the slope leading down to the mine workings, now unusually quiet. In sight also was the barbecue, burning fiercely with no one in attendance.

Or was there? Iron Eyes lay still. There was a slight movement behind the huge rain barrel that stood at the corner nearest to him — a glimpse of fair hair and the movement of a shoulder.

Within a moment, Iron Eyes recognized the hair and checked shirt of the young man called Andy, and knew he crouched there with his rifle, ready and waiting for a sight of the enemy.

Iron Eyes had the same distant

relationship with Andy as he had with Lewis's other men. An Indian employed to help with the horses and mules did not count for much in this mine and there was no pretence at friendship. He knew Andy as an arrogant young man without much common sense and inclined to be a little naïve. Often enough the youngster was made fun of, in a coarse way, by his companions. Iron Eyes had seen a pail of water hurled at Andy to the accompaniment of much merriment. He was not, in the opinion of the Osage, a wise man.

That did not mean he could not shoot well enough and Iron Eyes felt it to be a great risk to begin a rifle duel with his opponent in cover and knowing the first shots would attract the attention of Lewis. All was quiet for the moment and the Indian guessed both sides were lying low and trying to ascertain the whereabouts of the other.

It could be that Andy was not fully aware of what was happening. Iron Eyes could not recall seeing the young man at the other side of the house when the trouble started. It was just possible he would not quite realize who had pulled the snake-oil man out of trouble. The chance had to be taken . . .

Iron Eyes slid behind a thick pine, stood up, and then walked calmly into the open, rifle held in his hand but pointed to the ground. He believed that Lewis, from his crouching position by the side window, would not see him. There was no time to be lost.

He stepped firmly over the open space towards the rain barrel and then pretended surprise to see Andy half-rise with raised gun. The Osage smiled and lifted a hand in friendly greeting. He furrowed his brow as if puzzled.

'I hear shots. You have trouble? Bad men come?'

Andy was standing upright, his rifle barrel pointing a little to the left. He was staring at the Osage, recognizing him as a mine employee but uncertain as to his part — if any — in the fracas which had just broken out.

'Well, thing is . . . these guys . . . Hey, you oughta keep down! You could git sh . . . '

A knife flashed and struck as a snake strikes, with deadly accuracy. Andy gasped only once as the blade entered his heart.

Then the Osage moved like lightning. Both hands grasped blazing brands from the fire. He dashed to the open window and hurled them in, aiming deliberately at the oil-lamp standing on the deal table. It crashed over the polished surface and thumped to the floor. In a second the oil burst into flame and began to take hold of the silk screen by the fireplace. Iron Eyes ran again and returned with two more burning sticks which he threw further into the room. One fell upon the upholstered chair in which Lewis liked to rest his weary body; the other rolled blazing across the carpet.

Iron Eyes ran again and drew two more brands from the metal frame. His fingers blistered but he seemed unaware of it. His whole mind was intent upon his task. His hatred for Lewis smothered every other thought or feeling. He saw himself as being in the act of smoking out a wild beast as he had seen whites do with wolves or bears, with nothing but cruelty in their hearts. In his mind's eye, he could see Lewis already burning — or crawling outside to meet the same knife as had finished young Andy minutes before.

The room rapidly became an inferno as the fire was fed by air rushing in from both windows, set at either end for coolness in summer. The fine wooden panelling, tinder-dry from the long heat of the season, was blazing. The silk screen curled and smoked. The deal table and bureau were well alight. The dignified picture of Lincoln burned and fell . . .

In the next room, Lewis took a little time to react. He thought he had heard Andy's voice but had no idea to whom he could have been speaking. The strange thumps from the next room had puzzled him but he could not rush to the door and was not sure whether he ought to abandon his station by the window. Only when he caught a hint of smoke and heard the unmistakable rush of flame did he haul himself to his feet and hobble painfully over the little room.

The heat struck him as he opened the interior door and found himself confronted by a wall of flame in his parlour. All his furnishing blazed. Acrid smoke filled the air and caught at his throat. He grabbed at the edge of the door to steady himself as he began to lose his balance and it slammed shut behind his staggering body. Across the flaming bureau he could just make out the window to the rear of the house. There was a figure there, seeming to bob about in the smoke, with what appeared to be a burning brand uplifted and ready to throw. It looked like the head and shoulders of an Indian.

Lewis brought out his handgun as

swiftly as his stiff hands would allow and fired twice in quick succession. The figure vanished but Lewis, knocked off balance even further by the effort of firing the Colt, fell heavily to the floor. His trousers were in the flaming fuel on the carpet and immediately his clothing was alight.

He crawled as best he could for the window leading to the front of the house and put his hands up to grasp the sill, summoning all his will in a desperate attempt to pull himself up and topple outside . . .

On the same grassy stretch where Lewis now longed to be, Thady squirmed in his own struggle to hold on to life. The dark fog came and went over his mind. It was as if he had fallen into a pit and climbed with painful slowness towards the light only to fall back again. The mouth of the pit yawned before him and seemed to have become part of himself, for his face had become a cavern that tasted and smelled of blood and his life poured from it in a flood that could not be halted.

He was aware of pain and he was aware also of anger. It seemed that Lewis stood over him with a smoking gun. The bullet had ripped through his head and had carried his life with it. He did not know when this had happened or how, for such questions meant nothing in the darkness of death, but in the faint light that filtered into his mind, he sought to drag Lewis down with him.

He saw his hands outstretched on the bloody grass towards the butt of a handgun, the same gun as Lewis had given him at some unknown time in the past. He grasped it and looked through blood-covered eyes to the massive cliff which loomed in front of him. There he saw a square of burning light and a vague figure against it. He did not know for sure that he saw Lewis but he steadied his elbows against the ground and held the gun in both hands and pointed it in the direction of the square. He did not think further before pulling the trigger of the Navy pistol and sinking finally into the dark.

Lewis fell back. It was as if a weight of rock had fallen upon his chest. He knew his legs and back were burning and his lungs seemed to be drowning in blood but he could do nothing to help himself. Overhead, a blazing timber cracked and gave way . . .

In the pine woods nearby Sam heard the shots from the house and believed Iron Eyes to be in combat. Somehow, he did not believe the Indian could come off best in the face of Lewis and any of his men who were there. He had no idea the house was on fire until he heard a shout and saw a man in a black jacket and holding a rifle, rise incautiously from cover near the edge of the wood and point in the direction of the building.

Then the Choctaw fired and the man fell.

Within seconds a fusillade of shots

brought a shower of pine needles down upon them. It was obvious that there were men in the woods between themselves and the horses. There was no way of finding a way past them so they would have to be fought through.

'No sense in waiting,' said Karl. 'Best just push on.'

They did so, taking what advantage they could from the trees but expecting at any moment to be struck down by a red-hot bullet. Sam and Porcupine were a little in the lead while Karl held on to Julia's arm, all the time keeping his pistol in his left hand.

Suddenly they were face to face with the enemy. Four men appeared just ahead, partly concealed behind tree trunks, with rifles already pointing. A bullet sang past Sam's shoulder and he heard Karl grunt in pain. In return, the Choctaw fired twice and brought down a man in a red shirt who kicked twice only on the carpet of pine needles.

'Let's go for them!' yelled Karl and

darted forward, keeping his body between Julia and the enemy.

He fired and a man screeched, dropped his rifle, and held on to his stomach. Sam shot another in the leg and the Choctaw finished him as he staggered backwards.

For a moment, Porcupine struggled to reload and dropped behind. Sam felt a searing pain across his upper arm as a bullet grazed him. The blood flowed profusely, soaking his shirt. He discovered that he could no longer raise his rifle.

A man suddenly cursed and threw his empty rifle to the ground. He stepped into the open in a quick, brave gesture and Sam recognized him as the one who had stood beside Lewis when Thady was shot. The cold eyes were narrow and the mouth under the heavy moustache twisted in defiance.

'You again, Hendrix!' snapped Karl. 'I've seen you too often. Time to turn down the lamp!'

For a second it seemed they both hesitated. It was as if each could see death in the face of the other.

Then two handguns rose and pointed with no trace of a nervous quiver.

10

Both guns seemed to blaze at once but it was Hendrix whose body leaped in shock and fell over backwards. His head struck a low-hanging bough a glancing blow as he fell and there came no sound but a gasp from his gaping mouth. Blood suddenly gushed in a torrent from the wound in his chest as the artery from his heart burst and poured out his life. In a moment his shirt was a mass of red. His legs jerked for seconds only and then he was still.

'All men dead now,' said Porcupine, staring at the corpse.

'No! Look!' called out Julia, pointing into the shadows where she could see a figure some distance away, loping off in silence like a wolf, with head bowed under the branches.

The Choctaw did not hesitate but ran

in the same wolf-like manner in pursuit. He vanished into the trees but then reappeared minutes later, slipping his knife into its sheath.

'All men dead now,' he grunted.

His eyes were on Karl whose face was suddenly white and strained.

'I go for horse number four,' stated Porcupine. 'Two people no good for one horse.'

Before they could speak he was off again at a run, making towards the edge of the trees in the general direction of the house. The smell of smoke was now heavy in the air. Sam guessed that the Osage, Iron Eyes, had had much to do with it. Somehow, he felt the Indian had not survived.

'We need to git to the horses quick,' he insisted. 'Maybe that polecat Lewis and some of his guys are still around.'

They went on their way, hoping that memory was serving them well and that they were heading to the place where they had left their mounts. Karl walked steadily enough for some distance and then he stumbled and caught at his side.

'Hey, you all right?' asked Sam anxiously. 'You've been hit . . . I knew it!'

Blood was soaking the older man's clothing but he shook his head and pressed on with an increasingly shambling gait. A moment later they could see the horses tethered where they had left them.

'Karl! Karl, you must stop!' said Julia, her voice reaching a pitch of worry. 'Let's see that wound. Maybe I could do something.'

As soon as they reached the little clearing where the horses waited Karl slumped to the ground. Julia bent over him and pulled his shirt from his blood-covered side. The wound was deep and the blood flowing from it was dark. She knew at once that there was no hope but she pressed her hands against it in a forlorn gesture. The blood seeped between her fingers and she cried like a child at the death of its parent.

'I got . . . my . . . badge . . . ' Karl's voice was low, little more than a whisper. His hand had crept up to the lapel of his jacket and he stroked the little silver star once before his arm fell and he lay still.

Sam and Julia stood in silence.

They were unaware of the return of Porcupine who appeared a few minutes later leading a piebald pony. In one hand he held a black hat. For a moment he stood silently, then in a courteous gesture he put the hat on Sam's head.

'You wear medicine hat now. Wise old snake-oil man has gone away. Maybe this hat give you wisdom like him.'

He stood for a further moment in silence and then he slapped the piebald pony on the rump and watched it as it wandered over to the nearest patch of grass.

'Osage pony not needed now. Two Osage dead. Lewis all burned in his house. All bad men dead.' He looked gravely at Sam and Julia. 'You go away now pretty quick. Big smoke fire bring people up from Red Lance. They angry. Big boss dead. Work dead. Money dead. Angry people never listen. I go too.'

He swiftly mounted his own horse and began to turn away.

'Where to?' asked Sam.

'You go West,' answered the Indian, not quite understanding the question. 'I go to Choctaw nation. All too much trouble with whites.'

He rode swiftly by the edge of the trees and soon vanished from sight.

Sam knew the young Indian was right. There was too much of a mess here for explanations and the mine employees would be looking for someone to blame. If Sam and Julia rode off with all speed then who was to say they had ever been here?

He took Julia by the arm, drawing her away gently from where Karl lay.

'We need to go,' he said quietly. 'These folks, when they come, will give him a decent burial. We kin vanish. It's the best way.' He stood for one more moment, looking at the silver-star badge as it caught the sunlight. 'What do they call this mine? Starlight? This must be the first time it ever deserved its name!'

They rode on through the woods, descending by degrees to more open country. They rode through the night because they felt the need to put distance between themselves and the tragedy of the hillside. They rode in silence for they needed time to grieve . . .

Sometime during the next forenoon they stopped to rest the horses and to slake their thirst at a pure, glistening stream. Sam watched Julia as she knelt on the grassy bank and lifted a little water in the palm of her hand to her mouth. He noticed that she grimaced slightly as she did so and he knew she had pain in her arm. She caught his glance and smiled.

'It's a bit sore,' she admitted. 'Comes from shooting off that gun yesterday.

You were right about the recoil.'

He put out his hand in a quick, impulsive and tender gesture and touched her bad arm, his eyes showing his sympathy.

'It's all right . . . feels better every minute . . . Can't expect to get through a fight like that without getting hurt.'

'Yeah, I know,' he murmured. 'Life always hits you one way or another, whether it's in a fight or being in prison or whatever. We jest make the best of it. Leastways, most of us try to.'

Then they went on, their spirits somehow uplifted, their eyes drifting ahead over the sea of grass which was appearing before them.

'Thing is,' said Sam, more to himself than his companion, 'revenge ain't no good. Jest about everybody got their revenge back there but it jest ended up with one hell of a mess — if you'll pardon the expression.'

'You're pardoned.'

'Seems to me that you don't ever feel any better after revenge even when you think you've got it.'

'You're right — but that isn't always easy to learn. What really matters is making a life for yourself.'

'What we're goin' to do is to head straight out West for a while and then I'll git work — any kind of work — so long as it's straight. After that, I'll see if I kin make something of myself, only I'll do it fair and square.'

'Yes.'

'I could end up being somebody quite important in my own way.'

'Sure, but don't think because you're wearing that hat you'll be the big boss right away. I'm here too. Nobody bosses me.'

'I know it,' replied Sam grinning and sneaking a glance at her. 'Think you might marry me?'

'Could be,' she answered smiling, 'but it depends on you getting a job and going straight.'

'Sure thing.'

'Don't suppose I'll find anybody better anyway.'

We do hope that you have enjoyed reading this large print book.

Did you know that all of our titles are available for purchase?

We publish a wide range of high quality large print books including:
**Romances, Mysteries, Classics
General Fiction
Non Fiction and Westerns**

Special interest titles available in large print are:
**The Little Oxford Dictionary
Music Book, Song Book
Hymn Book, Service Book**

Also available from us courtesy of Oxford University Press:
**Young Readers' Dictionary
(large print edition)
Young Readers' Thesaurus
(large print edition)**

For further information or a free brochure, please contact us at:
**Ulverscroft Large Print Books Ltd.,
The Green, Bradgate Road, Anstey,
Leicester, LE7 7FU, England.
Tel:** (00 44) **0116 236 4325
Fax:** (00 44) **0116 234 0205**

He saw her eyes were bright and her smile belied the irony of her tone. He grinned and urged his horse on a little faster.

'Big deal!' he yelled suddenly. 'Let's go!'

THE END

Other titles in the
Linford Western Library:

BLIND TRAIL

Mark Bannerman

Whilst on military patrol for the United States Cavalry, Lieutenant Raoul Webster is blinded in a freak accident. Guided by his young brother, he sets out for San Francisco to consult an eye doctor. But, en route, their stagecoach is ambushed by ruthless Mexican bandits. Raoul's brother is murdered, as are the driver and all the male passengers. Raoul survives, but he is alone in the wilderness and vulnerable to all Fate can throw at him. He is kept alive by one burning ambition, to track down his brother's killer . . . .

SIX-SHOOTER JUNCTION

David Bingley

Deputy Sheriff Sam Regan considered he had been lucky when he found an outlaw's horseshoe mark outside the Bankers Hotel in Blackwood after a bank raid. He overtook a raider and was badly shaken to learn that the outlaw was Pete Arnott, a boyhood friend. The meeting, however, led to gun play and Sam had to kill Pete. He tried to hide the fact that Pete was an outlaw, but the truth leaked out to certain important people who insisted on Sam chasing the raiders and proving the link between Pete and the gang . . .